I0529739

Sloane's Solitude

by
Emmy Tidning

Applied Divination
Redmond

Sloane' Solitude
Copyright © 2023 Emmy Tidning
ISBN 978-1-959786-01-6

All rights reserved. No portion of this book may be reproduced or utilized in any form, or by electronic, mechanical, or other means, without the prior written permission of the publisher.

Published by Applied Divination
Edited by Emily Paper
Formatted for print by Applied Divination

This book is a work of fiction. If any part of Sloane's Solitude resembles the life of a known person, living or dead or currently in ghost form, it is entirely coincidental.

First printing edition 2023
Applied Divination
www.applieddivination.com

Dedicated to the spirits,
living and dead.

Also from Emmy Tidning

Faye's Fortune

When worlds collide and fortune-teller Faye reveals a dark secret about Jasper's relationship, will their fates prove to be destined, or doomed?

Charlie's Chill

For a smooth-talking, tranquility-touting Reiki massage therapist, Charlotte is anything but calm. Her business is barely scraping by, her partner is love-struck, her friend is paranoid, and she's somehow always in two places at once. Can a truck driver's son talk her down off the ledge, or has he got her all stressed out, too?

Find Fortune with Faith in *Faye's Fortune*
Chill out with Charlotte in *Charlie's Chill*

Applieddivination.com

CHAPTER ONE

The sound of keys clicking in the first of her three deadbolts made the hair on Sloane's arm shoot upward, prickling her flesh. At the second deadbolt, she grasped at her kitchen counter and sucked in a deep breath. As the third and final lock was cracked, she tensed her upper body and closed her eyes.

Charlie's voice echoed up the stairwell, "Hey you, it's me."

Sloane relaxed, draining her lungs of stale air, and letting her shoulders fall away from her ears. "I'm in the kitchen," her voice wavered back, and she continued her task of sorting through a myriad of boxes splayed out on her kitchen island.

Charlie tramped up the stairs in shiny knee-high black boots. Sloane figured she must have spent the day working as a cocktail waitress. Most days she was a masseuse, but that job required scrubs and sneakers. Sloane wondered how Charlie could do it all.

Smiling mischievously, Charlie pulled a bottle of Mount Pleasant Merlot from behind her back and set it on the counter across from Sloane.

"Borrowed this from the boss," Charlie winked and rounded the island, arms stretched out for a hug. "Did I scare you?"

"A bit, but it's getting easier," Sloane lied, holding her friend's hug for a few seconds too long. "You shouldn't steal booze. How was work today?"

Charlie ignored the admonition. She thought pensively before answering the question. "Crappy, actually, at both my massage studio and the bar. I don't know how to help Faith or Darius draw in more customers during these slower months. I can't believe this cleavage isn't attracting more gullible computer nerds." She looked down at her breasts.

"Hey, *I'm* one of those computer nerds," Sloane frowned and gawked at Charlie's boobs. "You do deserve a tip for those, though."

Her bestie continued, "I need to switch back to evening shifts and get them when they're staying late or pulling all-nighters." She opened a drawer near Sloane's stove and shuffled some kitchenware around. "If I worked evenings, I'd also have time for more massages during the day."

Charlie closed the drawer and opened another, but it was empty. A puzzled scowl formed on her face.

"Sorry, I can't find my corkscrew," Sloane confessed. She set down the box she'd been rifling through and picked up another one.

Charlie closed the drawer and put a hand on her hip. With the other, she waved at the boxes on the counter. "Damn, Sloane. You need to unpack this kitchen. You've lived here four weeks already." She took the first box Sloane had set aside, tucked it under an arm, and walked around Sloane's kitchen pulling cutlery and utensils out of it, placing them in random drawers.

"Hey!" Sloane forgot her own box and watched Charlie christen a drawer with tableware. "I haven't figured out the ideal kitchen setup yet!"

Charlie shrugged and pulled a heavily wrapped glass bowl out of the box.

"That's not kitchen," Sloane told her. "It's a breakable prop bowl from Brian's improv troupe."

"You stole a prop from your ex?" Charlie put the box back down on the island and unwrapped the package. It felt like a bowl and was almost as heavy as a bowl. Once unwrapped, she put it down on the counter. It busted into a handful of pieces.

Sloane gasped, mocking. "You don't realize how hard that is to put back together, woman!"

Charlie fidgeted with it, trying to stick the magnetized pieces together. "Where are you going to put this?"

"Maybe the front hall, I can put my keys in it and try not to break it when I do."

"Well, that's hardly a challenge. You never go anywhere so you don't need keys." Charlie managed to get the bowl back together and this time, she placed it down on the counter carefully. She tapped her long fingernails on the granite tiles and let her eyes lazily survey the rest of the space. "I see you got the TV up and a bookcase built. Who helped you?"

"Jose, one of the guys doing construction on the unit next door."

Charlie looked at her with twinkling eyes, and Sloane felt she should assuage any notion of potential romance. "No, Charlotte. He's not date-able material. He just happened to be installing the front steps next door, saw a few boxes delivered to my porch, and offered to help me move them in. I trust him, and he's cute, but there is no potential there. Or anywhere," Sloane bit her lip and continued to fumble through a box, sneaking a nervous look at her friend.

Charlie's eyes rolled and she mumbled something Sloane couldn't understand, then adjusted her composure. "Well, the living room furniture looks great. Now you just need to fill it with your stuff. Here," She knelt by a box on the floor, pulled five books out of it, and stood them on end on a bookshelf. Smiling proudly, she showcased her work. "You're slightly more moved in than you were two minutes ago! You're welcome."

Sloane pressed her lips together, unsure of whether or not she trusted anyone else to help decorate her personal space, but she accepted her friend's attempt to speed up the process of moving in.

"Oh, and look!" Charlie cheered, reaching back down into the book box. "Here's your corkscrew!"

Sloane smiled, recalling the day she'd packed it, her last day in the small house she shared with Brian in their Chicago condo. He'd moved the last of her stuff into his truck, opened a bottle to toast the end of their amicable split, and then wished for new beginnings for the both of them. Then, he'd driven the entire way to Jefferson City, Missouri, with Sloane hiding and panicked in the back seat. He was a real hero.

Sloane walked into the living room and took the tool from her friend. "Charlotte, you are nothing if not useful. Move in with me."

Charlie followed her back into the kitchen, rounding the other side of the island. She opened a few cabinets on the kitchen wall and quickly found what she was looking for.

She pulled two large wine glasses down. "I'm not moving in with you unless you deal with your issues. Your therapist would never forgive me for enabling you." She smiled as she said this, but her demeanor was serious. "Have you met with one here, by the way?"

Sloane busied herself opening the wine bottle, avoiding Charlie's eyes. "I spoke to my guy online when I first moved in. He's nice, but he says he can't work across state lines. Also he was too pushy anyway."

"He's supposed to be pushy, that's his job!" Charlie set the wine glasses in front of her friend and leaned her body onto the counter, bending to watch Sloane's face while she poured. Sloane stared into her task, expressionless. Charlie frowned and shifted her gaze thoughtfully toward the sliding glass doors next to the dining table and smiled. "Let's push it even further by sitting on the balcony."

Sloane finished pouring, looked toward the balcony doors, and flinched at the overwhelming world beyond. "I've already been out there to hang laundry today." She nodded toward the laundry basket on the floor of the dining room. "My dryer is broken."

"You'll have to take the dry laundry back in, then, correct?"

"I guess," Sloane relented. When her dryer problem began, she would hang the laundry around the dining room and leave the door open for the air to come in. When the weather became too cold, she opted to wait until nightfall on a cloudy day to venture outside, the darkness protecting her from seeing too much of the outside world.

Sloane looked toward the gray sky and wondered if she could go out there without suffering a full panic attack. Perhaps with Charlie here, she could.

She looked down at the wine glasses thoughtfully but left them where they were. As Charlie watched, Sloane took tentative steps into the dining room and picked up the empty laundry basket, nestling it protectively into her torso. She stood beside the balcony door like a puppy, not looking outside but instead watching Charlie, waiting for her to open the door and lead the way. Charlie smiled, grabbed a wine glass in each hand and approached the door, unlocking it with her pinky finger and sliding it open with her hip. She walked straight outside without pause. Sloane watched her in awe.

Just then, a wisp of fresh air blew in and scratched at Sloane's chest. She balked, closing her eyes and shifting slightly backward into the warmth of her home. She reminded herself that it was just air, it meant nothing.

She composed herself for the arduous journey outside.

"It's a new neighborhood," she whispered to herself. "There is probably nothing out there."

As she stepped out onto the patio, she permitted herself to look at the concrete terrace below her feet but stopped her gaze from straying beyond her towels hanging over the railing. She pretended the wrought iron bars were a protective barrier, made even safer by the drying linens shielding her from the breeze. Sloane kept her gaze within the confines of the small outdoor living area.

Two weathered director's chairs, monogrammed "Mason," were folded against the outside wall. Charlie set the wine glasses down near her feet and frowned at the embroidery as she began to unfold the first seat. "Why did you take Brian's chairs?"

Sloane had kept her maiden name, Jackson, all along, so why she'd claimed the outdoor chairs with her ex's name made little sense. As she set down her laundry basket and unfolded the second chair, she wondered how much it would cost to ship them back to the windy city.

She wasn't sure if Brian would want them back, anyway. To Charlie, she shrugged.

"How is Brian?" Charlie asked, as though sensing Sloane's thoughts about her ex-husband and the wayward chairs.

"I assume he's well," Sloane faced her chair away from the street and toward the sliding door, toward safety. "At least, I hope he's well. We still talk a little via text and email. Mostly practical stuff. 'How's your mom,' etc. That sort of thing." Sloane tucked her feet up under her body and stared at her knees. "We're friendly. I hope he's happy."

"How about you?" Charlie handed Sloane her wine glass.

"I hope I'm happy, too." Sloane did not continue the thought. She cocooned further into her chair and sipped her wine.

Charlie didn't sit in her chair right away. Instead, she leaned over the railing, first sweeping her gaze up and down the street and then over the surrounding townhouses, pausing at open curtains to look in on Sloane's neighbors. Sloane watched her friend's eyes but dared not follow their gaze. Instead, she glugged her wine, envious.

Charlie sipped her own glass delicately and sighed, "I need you back, Sloane. Where's my best high school gal pal?" She turned toward Sloane and softened into a grin. "I need someone to go out drinking with me on weekends!" She wiggled her shoulders, feigning a dance move.

Sloane giggled nervously. "We're out right now, and we're drinking! Isn't this enough?" She held up her glass and smiled, attempting to brush off the conversation.

"You're no fun," Charlie pouted. "Who is that?" She tilted her nose over the railing, looking into the road.

Sloane tensed. "Who is whom?"

"Handsome guy," Charlie whispered, "walking up the street."

"Is he looking at us?" *At me?*, Sloane meant but didn't say.

"No."

Sloane closed her eyes briefly and inched her body sideways, peering cautiously over the railing and onto the street. Her next-door neighbor Leonardo's blue Prius was parked in front of her house, a spot she'd offered him as she didn't have a car of her own. A black Bentley with tinted windows was further up the street. The plates were clearly not Missouri, but she couldn't read them from her location. Out of the corner of her eye she spotted the person Charlie had asked about, walking back from the mailboxes just outside her duplex.

"Oh, that's Jackson, he lives across the road." Sloane returned to facing into her house, where it was closed off, and safe.

"You're Jackson." Charlie's brow furrowed, but she continued to smile flirtatiously, probably hoping Sloane's neighbor would look up.

"No, Jackson is his *first* name."

"Oh, interesting." Charlie's tone became cute and flowery. "You two could get married and he could take your last name. Jackson Jackson."

Sloane smirked and rolled her eyes. The tension fell out of her shoulders, and she felt her anxiety wane. "Get this – his last name is Stone. I could be Sloane Stone and he could be Jackson Jackson."

"You're kidding," Charlie sat down in her chair.

For the first time, Sloane relaxed. She shrugged. "Besides occasionally getting his mail, I don't really know him that well. And anyway, I think he has some woman living with him."

"Oh, bummer." Charlie's body straightened into businesslike professionalism, turning off her flirting mechanism instantly. Sloane wished she could mimic her friend's skill at bizarre and magical nonverbal communication. Charlie asked, "You think she's a girlfriend?"

Sloane bit her lip. Honestly, she didn't even know if the woman was real. She didn't know if half of her neighbors were real. How much should she say?

"I see someone in his first-floor bedroom, but I don't know what their situation is."

Charlie eyed her. "And you don't know if she's a ghost."

Sloane's shoulders softened. She hadn't realized her whole body was tight, but she was glad to have a friend who understood. Or at least tried to understand.

Charlie laughed. "Well, you've clearly spied on him enough to track him and his roommate!" She raised her eyebrows mischievously and twisted her dark brown hair around her fingers. "If watching them has gotten you out on this porch, then you probably care more about him than you're letting on." She turned the flirt back on and leaned over the railing.

Out of the corner of her eye, Sloane saw Jackson turn at his door. Charlie waved at him. He looked at Charlie with a confused expression but waved up at the two of them. He smiled before entering his house.

Sloane watched him go in, then she turned away from the road again. She said nothing but felt a snag of envy at her friend's ability to be both flirtatious and harmless.

The soft sound of rattling tools resonated from the unfinished building next to Sloane's duplex--a sign that the construction workers were packing up for the day. The thickness of traffic on the main highway in the distance indicated that the rest of Suburbia was finished nine-to-fiving it, as well. As she sipped her wine, Sloane's comfort increased, and she braved a view of the street with her friend.

Living in a brand-new townhouse community was nice. It seemed that most of the people actually existed here, in the corporeal world. There aren't many dead in a brand-new development, Sloane reminded herself.

Unless it's build on an unknown ancient burial ground, she thought. She sucked in air at the notion.

"You're doing great, love," Charlie put a comforting hand on her leg, and they both watched the street and sipped their wine.

After Jackson, the neighbor from the duplex next to the Smythe's was the first to arrive home from work. Her small red Honda whirred erratically into the empty spot in front of Jackson's townhouse. Sloane thought she was some sort of school principal or other academic. Something Mackleby.

"Someone new move in next to the Pacillis?" Charlie's attention had moved from Jackson's front door to the duplex immediately next to Sloane's.

A woman stomped out onto their front porch with her arms waving, trying to get the principal's attention.

"What's her story?" Charlie asked, nodding in the direction of the woman.

"She and her weird husband Ken moved in about a week ago. The wife, Nina, has already declared herself the president of the homeowner's association. Honestly, this community doesn't even have enough residents to form a homeowners association yet." Sloane lowered her voice and fluffed a towel hanging on her railing. "She's been sending me notes about my laundry."

"It's amazing how you've only lived here for a month, you never leave, and yet you've already managed to get yourself into trouble," Charlie chuckled.

Nina's shrill voice echoed off the buildings across the street. "Mackleby, you need to park in front of your own house!"

Mackleby pretended not to hear Nina, and stormed into her townhouse right next door.

"Smart woman," Charlie laughed. "Who is Ken?"

"Honestly, I don't know much about him, I only ever see Nina ranting about my laundry, but I never see them together. I think he's some sort of software developer because if and when I do see him, he's always got a bag of chips and a laptop."

"Probably leaving just to avoid his wife," Charlie laughed.

The streetlights buzzed on and glinted off the mysterious black Bentley up the road. The hairs on Sloane's arm tickled her, and she wondered how long the driver had been in the car. Had he or she been watching them all this time? The car inched slowly out of the neighborhood, the top of the windows tinted too dark to see the driver's face, but Sloane noted it was a male.

As though sensing Sloane's thoughts, Charlie remarked, "He's probably considering a house in this area. Maybe he'll move into this empty unit right next to you!"

Sloane felt goosebumps forming on her arm, as she looked at the balcony connected to hers. It was an empty canvas with only a For Sale sign hanging from the railing, rattling in the wind. "I hope not. I'm enjoying not having a neighbor on my adjoining wall. If I get anyone half as loud as Francesca and Leonardo, or anywhere near as annoying as Nina, I'll cry."

"Francesca and Leonardo are these guys?" Charlie pointed her thumb at the quiet townhouse right beside them.

"Yes, they argue every morning. I hear it through my windows."

"Oooh, drama!" Charlie's eyes twinkled, "For someone who doesn't go anywhere, you sure know a lot about your neighbors."

"I keep notes, lest one of my neighbors turns out to be a ghost or a murderer." Sloane tried to be sarcastic, but she felt the rumblings of anxiety in her stomach.

Charlie rolled her eyes and looked toward the houses mirrored across the road. "Huh, looks like someone else has watchful eyes, too."

Sloane caught the blinds closing in the first-floor window of Jackson's townhouse.

Charlie took a sip of her wine and stared into the glass. "Your neighbor's girlfriend or buddy or-who knows what she is-was watching us."

Sloane stood and stumbled toward her sliding glass door, mumbling about the need to visit the bathroom. Charlie didn't argue, and instead followed her inside, giving Sloane a look of sincere pity.

Sloane was at least pleased that Charlie had seen the woman, because it meant she was a real, tangible human being. Nonetheless, it had been enough of the outside exposure. She decided she would remove the rest of her laundry in the morning, when any ghosts had gone to bed.

CHAPTER TWO

By ten that night, Charlie had long gone. To Sloane, the darkness felt heavier and more lonesome than usual. Usually more power conscious, this evening she opted to leave the main floor lights on as she walked upstairs to her master suite. In the bathroom, she stripped off her clothes and dropped them on the floor, kicking them carelessly into a corner. She climbed into a hot shower and stood still, allowing the drops to caress her flesh. She hoped the steam would calm her nerves and clear her foggy head.

Between them, she and Charlie had finished two bottles of wine. Not wanting to wake up with a hangover the next morning, Sloane decided the best thing to do after her shower was to stay awake long enough to drink a few glasses of herbal tea and unpack some more boxes. The mild calorie expenditure would hopefully help burn away the alcohol in her blood stream.

After toweling off, she shuffled her legs into PJ bottoms and pulled one of Brian's Notre Dame University sweatshirts over her head. She loved the feel of its fleece and hadn't been able to find a similar one from her own alma mater, Northwestern. *Or maybe*, she thought to herself, *I just kept his things as a reminder of better times.* As she pulled the soft fabric over her skin, she wondered if Brian missed his sweater, too.

Perhaps she wouldn't tell him she had it. She'd keep the outdoor chairs, too.

A loud knock echoed through the house. Sloane's heart leapt out of her chest, as though racing toward an exit that didn't exist. She felt the organ trying to bust out from behind her breast, and she had trouble collecting air into her lungs. She had no clue who could be at her door, and she froze in place, willing her pounding heart not to give her position away.

The knock sounded again, lighter this time and with a set pattern - *shave and a haircut, ten pence.*

Strangely calmed by the childish knock, she threw on a robe and descended the two stories to the front door. She desperately wished she had a peephole or some sort of window looking out onto her front porch. Not that she'd ever look out there willingly.

As loud as she could, she whispered, "Who is it?"

A male voice whispered back. "Hey Jackson, it's Jackson. From across the street."

Sloane's heart slowed, and she undid the first of the three deadbolts.

"You frightened me." She forced a careful smile as she undid the second deadbolt.

She heard Jackson chuckle lightly, "You're frightening me with all these locks." His grin could be heard from behind the door.

She started to feel embarrassed over the gratuitous locks she'd installed on the first day she moved in.

It's not as if they helped her agoraphobia. And if an apparition appeared, what would a lock even do?

She twisted the third and final lock and opened the door, backing away quickly from the outside world to let him in, then shut the door even faster behind her guest. She attempted to calm her panicked lungs and tried to disguise her stress with excess friendliness. "What can I do for ya, neighbor?"

'Ya?' She shook her head at herself.

Jackson jumped as the door was slammed shut behind him, but he adjusted himself smoothly. "I remembered I had some of your mail." He handed Sloane a stack of envelopes. "I would have come over sooner, but your friend was here, and I didn't want to interrupt you two. I hope this isn't too late."

"Not at all," Sloane lied. She would have preferred he'd come over earlier, only so that Charlie could answer the door. "Thanks for the special knock, by the way."

"I'm sorry if I scared you," Jackson's statement was sincere, but Sloane wondered if he was maybe a bit proud of himself for wielding such power over her. It was hard to tell with people. She knew so few of them.

She tested her theory with a joke, "Everyone scares me, don't go thinking you're special."

Jackson smiled but gave nothing away.

"Let me get the mail *I* have for you." Sloane moved toward a table in the hallway and flipped through some paperwork, grabbing anything labeled with his name instead of hers.

Jackson pointed at the glass dish on the table. "Nice bowl."

"Don't touch it!" Sloane said quickly. Jackson pulled his hand back, and she bit her lip. "Sorry. It's, uh, not real. It's just really awkward to put back together if it breaks."

Jackson gave her a puzzled look but didn't say anything. Sloane handed him a stack of stuff with his name on it.

"You can always leave this on my doorstep," Jackson waved the mail. Then his eyes wandered around the rest of her first floor. Sloane became conscious of how cold and ignored it was, because of how little time she spent in it. The walls were unpainted, the furniture sparse, and--save for the unusable fake-glass bowl--there was no décor on the floor whatsoever. Beyond her hall table, the townhouse's first floor bedroom was completely empty and white, with only the builder-grade vertical blinds half-open across the back window. She watched Jackson's hazel eyes drift that way, his eyebrows folded in confusion.

"Then we wouldn't be able to have this pointless banter," Sloane did her best teasing in order to pull his attention away from the unused room. She found the last of his mail in her stack and handed it to him. "If I were to leave your mail on your doorstep, I wouldn't see your scary face at 10pm."

She smiled, trying to quell the last of her jittery nerves. It was fun to have a similar name as her handsome neighbor, but she did hope the mailman got their mailbox units correct soon. She had trouble coming up with excuses for why she held onto his mail for so long. Asking Charlie or Jose the construction worker to drop it off at Jackson's house would only lead to more questions from everyone.

Jackson's attention returned to her. He shook off his early confusion at the almost unlived-in first floor. "Again, I'm sorry about the hour."

"It's fine. I have more unpacking to do and laundry to bring inside. This is a welcome distraction."

"I've been wondering about your laundry," Jackson said, "I'm surprised Nina Smythe hasn't sent you an infraction notice." He nodded his head in the direction of the duplex next door.

"Oh, she has," Sloane grabbed a pink 8x11 sheet of paper off the table and waved it at him. The words 'HOA Infraction' were printed boldly across the top in Comic Sans font. Sloane shook her head and smiled, "I just ignore them. What else can I do? My dryer is broken."

Jackson chuckled. "I get those for parking my car in front of the wrong house." As he backed toward the front door, he offered, "You're always welcome to bring your laundry over and borrow our dryer."

Sloane smiled, careful not to take note of the word 'our,' although her curiosity was more than piqued about that mysterious woman. "It's okay, I get cheap thrills from pissing Nina off."

"A woman after my own heart," Jackson winked, and pushed down the door handle to open it.

Sloane felt a gust of outside air and her heartbeat grew louder in her ears. She straightened her body and ignored his tease, her senses frozen in fear.

Jackson's face soured and he pulled the door open wider. Sloane stared at his feet, trying to maintain composure, but failing miserably. A bead of sweat formed on her brow.

Jackson gave her a strange look but said his goodbyes quickly and walked out.

Sloane closed the door to within an inch, heaved a breathy "goodbye" and then shut it hard behind him, hating herself for being unable to flirt back while exposed to the outside like that. She secured the door handle and rapidly slammed each deadbolt, locking the spirits out for another night.

She hoped.

CHAPTER THREE

It was well after midnight when Sloane finished unpacking the rest of the kitchen. The routine had calmed her enough, she felt, to retrieve the rest of her laundry from outside. Still, she paced back and forth in front of the balcony door and ultimately couldn't bring herself to open it. She went upstairs to her room and, for a while, she lay in bed staring at the ceiling, but sleep evaded her. When it became apparent that she'd be awake for a few hours yet, she plodded downstairs to sift through her book boxes.

As she stacked books on her shelf, she delighted in the feeling of permanence that having full bookshelves brought. She became lost in the process of perfectly aligning the bindings and creating a livable haven for herself.

Nearing three in the morning, she loaded the washer upstairs with a few tablecloths she'd found amongst the boxes in her living room, and she felt even more domestic and ready to begin building her home the way she needed it. She toyed with the idea of using the empty first floor room as a large walk-in closet—a décor plan that otherwise might be the dream of a single gal finding her way in the world--but she decided the main floor was too exposed for comfort.

Whatever this mental illness was, it meant she wasn't a typical single gal. This thought dispirited her, and she leaned back against her washing machine, wishing the dryer would magically start working. She needed help.

A sharp female scream echoed between the townhouses, and Sloane instinctively dropped to the floor.

CHAPTER FOUR

Thinking it might be Francesca going into labor, Sloane dared to stand and look out at her next-door neighbor's townhouse. If she avoided looking at the street, she'd be safe.

But none of the lights at Francesca and Leonardo Pacilli's duplex appeared to be on. Sloane walked quietly downstairs to the second level, sucked in a breath, and peered out through the sheer curtains of the sliding glass balcony door.

She couldn't see anything. Nervously, she took a deep breath and held it, opening the balcony door. She let the cool air sweep in and she adjusted her composure. At first, she slid only her upper torso outside to peek further onto the street. She wished Charlie were here to tell her what was real and what was imagined. Was the scream from a real person? Do ghosts even scream?

There were still no lights on anywhere in the Pacilli's house. The Smythe's house on their other side was relatively dark, but the front porch light was on. The entire duplex next to that was dark as well. The only lights on in the neighborhood belonged to Jackson's first floor room, and one flickering recessed light in the unfinished duplex attached to Sloane's. Most of her neighbor's cars were in their correct parking spots except

Jackson's black sedan, which was parked further up the road from his house. The assigned parking space in front of his house was empty.

There was no one out, thank goodness. If ghosts were around, they weren't out that night.

Sloane saw Jackson's front door open. She tucked her body against her balcony door frame, trying to make herself physically smaller. She wished she'd had the forethought to turn off her main floor lights before opening the balcony door, so she could hide in the shadows.

Jackson appeared in his doorway. He bent his upper body out to look up and down the street, then wandered out down his front steps. Sloane noted he was shoeless, his footsteps not making a sound on the cement.

Sloane watched him move silently up the sidewalk, peer into his car windows, then look back at the empty parking spot in front of his house, scratching his head. He shifted his gaze around the quiet townhouses with their lights turned out, and then his eyes came to rest on Sloane in her brightened balcony doorway.

"Hey." He moved toward her house and called softly, "Did you hear that, too?"

She bent further out her door, relieved that she wasn't imagining the scream. "I did."

"Wasn't you?"

"You're not that scary, Jackson," she tried to kid him.

Jackson chuckled, but it was hard to see his face in the dark. "Did you see anyone?"

Sloane shook her head, "Not since earlier." She recalled the woman spying on her and Charlie from Jackson's main floor. "I saw someone in your window around nine."

"This window?" Jackson pointed at his first floor.

Sloane nodded, then realized that in the dark he might not be able to see her movement. "Yes," she said carefully, then hoped to the gods she wasn't seeing dead spirits in Jackson's main floor. If they could enter his house, could they enter hers?

But Charlie had seen her too. She was a real person, Sloane reminded herself.

"Oh," Jackson's voice pulled her out of her fear. "That's my cousin, Alanis. I haven't seen her in a few days, though."

"You must have just missed her," whispered Sloane. Out of the corner of her eye, Sloane spotted a lamp move within the unfinished half of her duplex. She backed her body up and clutched the sliding door handle.

Jackson looked from his car to his house, muttering. "Odd that she didn't say hello before she left again." He seemed to say this more to himself than to Sloane.

A light popped on at the Smythe's townhouse and the door opened, revealing Nina's slender body. She crossed her arms in front of her torso and shouted about Jackson's car. Sloane backed the rest of the way into her house and inched the sliding glass door closed. This was too much extrovert behavior for one day. Even *live* people were starting to be too much.

From within her dining room, she watched Jackson approach Nina and the two seemed to bicker for a moment, waving their hands at his car.

Eventually, Nina retreated into her house. Jackson appeared to look up at Sloane's balcony, but not seeing her he went back into his townhouse. Within minutes, all lights were back off in the neighborhood.

Sloane locked her balcony door and sunk to the floor. It was all too much yet again. This time, before retiring upstairs, Sloane turned off all of her lights.

The next morning, a body was discovered in the trunk of Jackson's car.

CHAPTER FIVE

A mild headache greeted Sloane when she awoke at six. Shortly after she'd hid from Nina's view, she'd headed for bed to try and get as much sleep as possible. Three hours was certainly not great, but was enough to kill off the last of the wine and give her something to go on. She planned to nap after work to catch up. Napping worked just as well as sleeping anyway, her dislike of the outdoors having taken hold of her life so mercilessly during the day.

A six o'clock wakeup gave her plenty of time to shower and drum up the mental energy required to log in to the boring government servers, for another day of mindless admin work.

She took a quick look out her bedroom window but didn't see any movement at the Pacilli's house across the alley. Perhaps Leonardo had left for work early and Francesca slept through it, or maybe they were taking these last few weeks of Francesca's pregnancy to finally stop arguing and get some good sleep. Sloane wondered if she'd grown to welcome their arguing voices in the morning. Perhaps their loving but loud spats helped ease the loneliness of hiding at home.

Flickering red and blue lights caught her attention from the front of the alley, and she darted towards her office window to gain a better view. There was no mistaking cop cars. Ghosts didn't flash blue and red lights at her.

Three cop cars, all eerily silent but with flashing lights, surrounded Jackson's black car.

She couldn't see what was happening from her top floor, so she grabbed her housecoat from a hook on the bedroom door and moved downstairs to the dining room to brave the balcony.

She inched open the sliding glass door and peered out carefully, letting the cool air tickle her nervous cheeks, her hairs already on end. She could have sworn she felt a cursed energy penetrate her pores, as though she'd just let in a demon.

She admonished herself. *Cops aren't* that *bad, Sloane.*

Sloane pulled the knot on her housecoat tight and slipped her second bare foot out onto the cold concrete, trying to quench her shiver so as to not be noticed.

Three or four officers stood beside Jackson's car. Jackson was speaking to another officer on her side the road, in front of the Smythe's house. A large man Sloane didn't recognize stood on a porch further down the street, in one of the newly built houses. He didn't seem to see Sloane, which gave her comfort. A tiny dog stood at his ankle.

Nina stood on her balcony with her hands on her hips, just above Jackson and the police officer. Sloane watched her leaning over her railing, clearly trying to overhear the conversation.

The blinds in Jackson's first floor moved slightly, as though pushed by a breeze from inside his house. Sloane took one step back into her dining room.

Maybe Alanis is home, she calmed herself.

Jackson appeared distraught, and the officer serious.

A deep and accented voice asked, "Do you know what that is about?"

Sloane startled and jumped all the way backwards into her dining room. Her heart leapt out of her chest, and she started coughing like an automatic reflex.

She shook her head, found her composure, and snuck a peek back out the dining room doors, turning to the right. On the unfinished balcony which abutted hers, a construction worker stood staring at her.

"Jose," she breathed out, dropping her shoulders and relaxing against the doorframe.

Jose waved and grinned, sheepishly. "Sorry Ms. Jackson."

She stepped outside carefully, her brain trying to gauge the safety of venturing closer to him.

Although Jose had seemed a little nervous at her leap, he waited with patience and smiled at her with kindness.

She forced herself away from the safety of her sliding doors and walked toward their joint railing. Long term, she knew it would help to have one of the construction workers on her side, were she to need more help hanging shelves, bringing in items, or getting her mail. Jose seemed safe enough for that.

"I'm s-sorry about that," she stammered, pointing a chin back at her balcony door where she'd just bolted, like a teenage victim in a horror movie. "You startled me."

Jose held his hands up as an unspoken apology for frightening her. He gestured at the police scene up the street.

Sloane answered his original question. "I don't know what that's all about. What can you see from there?"

Jose shrugged but didn't seem eager to step forward and look closer. He actually took a step back, seeming as if he were hiding behind Sloane.

The two of them watched Nina leave her balcony, and soon she was out her front door, advancing toward the commotion. She began to step down and speak forcefully, "What's going on out—"

A police officer spotted her and held up a hand, shouting, "Sorry ma'am, no further."

Another officer pulled thick yellow tape out of the trunk of one of the squad cars, and walked toward a streetlamp between Jackson's duplex and one next door.

Uh-oh, thought Sloane, *this is serious.*

Further up the street, Sloane watched the large man huff and pad back into what must be his new house.

"Do you know that man?" She asked Jose.

"New neighbor. Ricardo, I think. He lives alone. I just installed new Moen faucets in his duplex!" Jose beamed in pride, appearing to forget about the melee below them.

At the sound of his voice, an officer spun around, the morning sunlight in her eyes.

Jose seemed to jump. "I have to get back to work," he said hurriedly, and before Sloane could say anything he had bolted back inside the connected townhouse.

The officer looked up, held a hand above her eyes to block out the light, and spotted Sloane. Sloane twitched, eager to also get the hell back inside her house.

"Ma'am, can I ask you a few questions, please?"

Sloane nodded, her breath starting to catch in her throat, and the overwhelming vastness of space swallowing her tiny body whole. "I'll come downstairs," she squeaked.

She looked once more for Jose, but he was long gone. The for-sale sign seemed to twist in the vacant space he'd left behind. *Did I imagine him?*

Sloane ran into her house and bolted the balcony door closed, shutting the transparent sheers as though they made any difference in keeping the light out.

I hope this officer doesn't expect me to come outside. How would I explain myself? Sloane thought this frantically, as she took careful but rapid steps down the staircase. She peered into the empty room on her first floor and didn't see anything out of the ordinary.

She unlocked the first of three deadbolts, and her breath became labored.

At the second lock, she heard a noise behind her door, someone was coming up the stairs.

"No, no, please not today," she whispered to herself.

A light knock pattern sounded. Not *shave and a haircut*, but something else, like a jazz beat.

She opened the door and let the woman inside, shutting it behind her and trying not to slam it.

"This isn't necessary, ma'am," The officer pulled out a notebook and scribbled something. "We can stand outside."

"I can't," Sloane's shoulders dropped. "I have ag- condition." She'd almost said agoraphobia. *It's not agoraphobia*, her inner monologue wanted to scream. *It's a crippling fear of the dead. Or maybe the undead. Or maybe anyone and anything in general.* "My name is Sloane," she finally said.

The officer eyed her but didn't dig deeper into Sloane's mental health. Instead, she just wanted to know who else lived in the neighborhood.

"Besides your neighbor Nina Smythe, whom I've already met-" the officer's eyebrows folded but she wiped the look away quickly. "And Mr. Stone across the street."

Sloane told her who she knew about, but left Jose out of it. Something was off about the way he'd just left, and she didn't want to get him in any trouble. She was also starting to wonder if he was real.

No, he must be. He hung my TV.

The officer was writing down names. "And can you tell me where you were the past few nights?"

At this, Sloane relaxed. She never went anywhere so she recounted the evenings of unpacking boxes, and then her friend Charlie coming over for wine. She'd neither left her house nor saw anything interesting in the neighborhood. She didn't like to look outside. None of it was a lie.

"And this friend, Charlie? Can we get her information too to confirm?"

Sloane worried her lip. What was going on? She gave the officer her friends' number and prayed Charlie was okay.

Giving no other details, the officer thanked Sloane for her time and said another officer would be along later to ask further questions. "You work from home, ma'am?"

"I do," Sloane answered.

"Good. Please don't go too far in the next few days, if possible."

Sloane shrugged, she couldn't go anywhere, to be honest.

Letting the officer back outside, she snuck a peek at the street scene over the woman's shoulder. As one officer moved away from the back of Jackson's car, Sloane caught sight of a woman's bloody leg and died red hair, folded awkwardly inside the trunk.

Alanis.

She gasped and slammed the door.

CHAPTER SIX

Sloane stared at the back of the door for what felt like a solid minute. Then, she bolted upstairs to the main floor, wishing there was another door in the townhouse that she could slam and triple-deadbolt. Eventually, she settled on huddling on the sofa in her living room at the back of her house, clutching her chest in disbelief at what she'd just seen. She huffed huge gasps of her home's stale but safe air.

Jackson's roommate was dead.

Jackson's roommate was dead in Jackson's trunk.

Who even was Alanis, anyway?

What had happened to her? Did it happen last night?

A foggy recollection of the night before tried to push its way through Sloane's cognition, but to no avail. The wine and exhaustion had wiped out most of her coherent thought.

A knock at the door tore a small shriek from her lips. The hairs on her arm shook, and she clutched the wristbands of her robe, tearing her short but trim nails into the wool.

She could see a faint reflection of the red and blue light softly shining through her dining room shears. She felt at least a little bit safe knowing there was a crowd of living police officers just outside her door. Perhaps the woman officer was back to ask more questions. She hadn't asked enough, in Sloane's opinion.

Sloane crept down the staircase wishing she had a peephole.

She opened the three locks and dared to peek out the doorway but saw no one. So strange. She was sure she'd heard a knock, but maybe she was imagining things. It was a lot, mentally, having the police in her neighborhood and people chatting with her. It's possible her brain was playing tricks on her. In the past day, it felt like she'd spoken to more people in person than she had since she moved in four weeks prior.

She opened the door wider and did her best to peer out into the street, where police were still surrounding Jackson's car. She dared not look in it, lest she see Alanis's leg again.

She didn't see Jackson in front of Nina's house anymore, nor the cop who had asked her questions after speaking with him. She wondered where they'd gone.

A slight breeze tickled her cheek, and she gasped and slammed the door, locking the deadbolts out of their regular order.

"Jesus Christ, Sloane," she said to herself aloud. "You are such a chicken shit."

"I'll say," whispered a voice behind her.

Sloane spun around and screamed. Standing in the doorframe of her first-floor bedroom was an almost opaque human form.

"Alanis," Sloane gasped, then her world went dark.

CHAPTER SEVEN

Sloane's head pounded, but there didn't seem to be any headache pain. She shook out the mental cobwebs and realized she'd been unconscious; she wondered for how long. The knocking continued, and it took her a minute to realize it was coming from the front door right next to her head. She'd awoken on the cold, tile floor of her front hallway.

There didn't appear to be anyone, real nor corporeal, in the room with her.

"Coming," she groaned, and pulled herself to standing. She unbolted the deadbolts and peered through the crack in the door. A handsome man stood there, and Sloane's shoulders relaxed. She was sure this one was real, as she'd noted he was wearing a police uniform. It was a safe bet he was a legit, living, human police officer.

She forced her shoulders to relax, and reminded herself that the world was a safe place, and that she had not been harmed.

All the same, she *did* need to make sure it was only one person, and not a massive collection of officers plus Jackson plus Jose plus a vision of Alanis again, swarming into her house and terrifying her into catatonia.

Before opening the door fully, she asked, "Can I help you?"

"Ma'am, my name is Officer Byrd."

Sloane took a breath. Meeting new people was not her favorite thing to do, but he was an officer of the law, and she felt she had a duty to respond to him.

"May I see your badge," she asked through the crack in the door. As though needing to explain herself, she finished the request. "I mean, that is, if you don't mind."

Officer Byrd's eyebrow went up, but he fumbled in his pocket and held what looked like a badge up to the crack. It was hard to read with one eye through a tiny slit.

"Thanks," she offered, and widened the crack at a snail's pace.

As she opened the door to him, she peered up and over his shoulders, watching for extra unexpected guests. Seeing none, she allowed Officer Byrd to step inside, and she shut and triple-locked the door behind him.

His body seemed to tense up, as though he felt trapped inside her house.

"I'm sorry," was all she offered.

He puffed out his chest, either to show off or prove toughness, she wasn't sure, so she ignored it. He pulled a notepad out of his breast pocket. "As I said, I'm Officer Byrd. I heard a noise and wanted to check in. I thought I could ask you a few questions, too."

"The other officer already asked me questions," Sloane said. She didn't say anything about the noise, she hadn't realized she'd made one.

She stole a brief glance toward the first-floor bedroom doorway, wondering if Alanis's dead soul was still hovering in there. Had she seen it at all, or was it all imagined?. Her brain could do wilder things, she reminded herself.

Officer Byrd noted her eye twitch and followed her gaze. "Do you mind if I look around," he asked.

Sloane was puzzled. "Do you need a warrant or something?"

"I don't know, *do* I?" He winked at her.

Now she wasn't sure what was happening. Was she under suspicion of whatever the hell was going on outside? Or was he flirting with her? Or both?

Suddenly overwhelmed with too much action for the day, Sloane said, "Can we make this quick? I have to get ready for work."

Officer Byrd seemed to forget about the bedroom and posed with his pen and notebook at the ready. "I just want to understand what happened last night."

Irritated by being drilled again, Sloane realized the officers were probably trying to catch someone in a lie. She thought hard trying to remember what she'd said to the other officer, the fainting having put her memories in a bit of a fog. "I had a friend over," she offered. "We sat on the balcony for a bit but didn't see anything at that time. I think I saw the dead girl, Alanis, in Jackson's house. Maybe around nine."

"How do you know the body we discovered was Alanis?"

"I-" Sloane thought for a second. How *did* she know? Besides the fact that she saw a woman's leg in the car, and an identical apparition had terrified her just a few minutes ago. She tried to avoid looking at the empty bedroom again. "I just assumed. I'm sorry, I don't actually know for sure."

"I see," Officer Byrd wrote something on his notepad.

"That's all I remember," Sloane offered a little too quickly. She felt a vague sense that some piece of information was missing, but she couldn't quite remember what else there was. The wine from last night had made things hazy.

"How much do you know about your neighbor, Jackson — uh," he rifled through his notepad for Jackson's last name.

"Stone," she interjected. "But beyond that I don't know anything."

"His name is Jackson Stone, and your name is Sloane Jackson?" Officer Byrd flipped through his notepad as though it held the secrets to the baby name universe.

"It was a surprise to both of us."

"So, you chat a lot?"

"No," Sloane said quickly. "In fact, we've barely said anything to each other. Everyone in this neighborhood has only recently moved in. But sometimes the postal service confuses our names, that's all."

"So," Officer Byrd looked back at his notes. "You know nothing about him? Can I ask what kind of name is Sloane? It sounds Russian." The cop fumbled with his pen and stood poised to write down anything she said.

"It's Irish," she was beginning to fume a bit. What did he care about her name?

"And Stone, you think that's Irish too?"

Sloane stared at him. "Jackson Stone?" No, I think it means rock."

Officer Byrd suddenly looked a bit embarrassed. Sloane watched a bead of sweat form on his brow, and felt justified, but also sympathetic. He was trying to solve a murder, after all.

She tried to get off the subject of names. "Look, I don't snoop through his mail, I just save it for him. I don't know much about him at all."

This was true, and she felt instant regret about it. She didn't know anything about the kind stranger who sometimes brought her misplaced mail. There'd been a few harmless flirtations and she sometimes wondered if the mail thing was truly an accident or an excuse for him to visit, but she'd never asked further than that about her handsome, across-the-street neighbor. She certainly wasn't hoarding *his* mail as any excuse to flirt. She literally didn't like being outside. But beyond the awkward mail trading every once in a while, she'd never asked Jackson anything about himself, nor had she inquired as to who Alanis was. She didn't even know where he worked, or how he spent his days.

Officer Byrd watched her carefully.

She took a moment to think hard about the kinds of mail he received, as it was the only clue she had to who Jackson Stone was.

"He has All State insurance," she held a finger up. "He donates to Make-a-Wish. He may subscribe or he once subscribed to a Cheese of the Month club. He still gets spam coupons from them and I often think about swiping them." Sloane blushed. Was it wrong to talk in front of a police officer about stealing a neighbor's coupons?

Officer Byrd smiled and jotted down a note.

"I can't think of anything else," she insisted.

The officer didn't question her any further on Jackson's mail or Sloane's coupon filching. He handed her a card with his name: Drew Byrd. "If you're sure you're okay, Ms-"

"Sloane is fine."

"Please contact me." He winked at her and added, "any time."

Sloane stopped herself from flinching. She did not feel like flirting with a police officer investigating a murder across the street, handsome as he was. She opened the door, and as she did, the other squad car drove out of the neighborhood carrying Jackson in the back seat. His hands were over his eyes and his entire body was slumped.

Sloane's jaw dropped. Officer Byrd's upper arm graced her shoulder and the hairs on her arm shot up. She suddenly felt like a cruel disease was spreading up her forearm, and she yanked her arm back. She longed to slam the door shut.

Officer Byrd sensed her nervous tension. "Taking him in is just protocol, Ma'am. We need to ask him a few more questions and it's easier to do it downtown."

He'd confused her reflex for concern for her neighbor, rather than the outside world which was beginning to flood into her door like a tsunami. This strange cop was now infringing on her personal space and breathing her air. She willed him out the door.

Officer Byrd nodded toward the retreating cop car. "We may come back with more questions, so make sure you stick around, please."

"I'm always around," she whispered, scanning the street and willing the man to move hastily out of her personal space.

He seemed to pick up on the ejection. "You have my number," he stated flatly, then tipped his cap as he exited her house. "If you think of anything I need to know, please call me.

Call me any time. I can be here in ten seconds," he seemed to laugh at himself.

Sloane smiled weakly and closed the door behind him. She scrambled up the stairs to find her phone, and she called in sick to work for the rest of the day. Even though she worked remotely, a murder across the road was too much for anyone's morning.

She threw herself onto her sofa and wondered if her old therapist's office in Chicago would take an emergency appointment, but then remembered that they can't work across state lines. Instead, she threw an arm over her forehead and leaned back onto the cushions.

"I thought he'd never leave," an echo sounded from somewhere nearby.

Sloane jumped and almost screeched again but pressed her lips together. She rose slowly to follow the voice.

Standing breezily near the dining room sheers, a mist resembling Alanis seemed to stare out at the street. Then it turned toward Sloane and tilted its head with a wide grin.

CHAPTER EIGHT

"Hello, neighbor," Alanis' voice echoed through Sloane's house. It almost sounded like it could come from anywhere, and Sloane wondered if she'd even seen the lips move. The apparition appeared to hold its wan smile.

Sloane folded her lips between her teeth, not quite sure how to respond.

After a few seconds, Sloane asked, "How'd you get in here?"

Alanis's head turned back toward the window, out to where the cops were surely wrapping up their detective work. "Get in here," her hollowed voice seemed to parrot. The apparition appeared to laugh, but no sound came out.

Sloane took a few tentative steps forward. Her fists were clenched to her sides, as though mentally prepping for another jump scare. She'd seen ghosts before, wandering the streets, but far more often when she lived in the older home with Brian. In Chicago, bodies were everywhere, living and non-living.

She thought the freshness of a brand-new townhome community would protect her from spirits entering her living space. She thought the isolation of being on the outskirts of town would keep them at bay.

She thought the deadbolts would lock them out.

She liked her deadbolts. She'd keep them, she thought to herself, trying to breathe through the fear of Alanis' apparition. At least they kept out the living.

Sloane moved around the dining room table to the left side of the patio doors. Alanis's ghost remained floating in the corner to the right, watching the outside world.

"You can call me Sloane," Sloane croaked. It was clear she was scared. She wondered if she was going insane, introducing herself to a dead person.

"Sloane." Alanis' voice parroted again.

"The locks keep regular people out, too." Sloane felt it important to justify why she had deadbolts on her door, when they probably didn't work for ghosts. Moving into a brand-new house hadn't worked either. Would anything?

"Regular people?" Alanis' voice bounced off the wall behind Sloane. The apparition's lips didn't move when she spoke.

"Y-you know," Sloane straightened her back, "I mean not dead."

"Dead?" The apparition's voice tilted upwards in its echo, questioning.

"I'm sorry, I th-thought you knew. It's what this is," Sloane looked from Alanis to the scene outside, then back again. She waved her hand in the general direction of Jackson's car, trying hard to keep herself together.

In her brief switch from staring at Alanis, she noticed that the coroner's van had arrived. The scene was blocked by officers trying desperately to keep out the looky-loos, but she assumed the body was being moved now.

She wondered if the ghost would follow the van that held her dead body, or would it stay in Sloane's house. If so, for how long?

Alanis's apparition seemed immobile. Sloane turned her attention to the outside world again.

Nina Smythe stood, horrified, on her front porch. The Pacillis huddled by Leonardo's car. Francesca clutched at her very pregnant stomach as though protecting her unborn fetus from the shock of a dead body.

Out of the corner of her eye, Sloane noted a movement and turned toward Alanis again. The apparition seemed to drift backwards from the window, through the dining room table and into Sloane's kitchen.

The fear dissipated. Sloane figured if Alanis could drift through tables and doors, any harm she might try to cause Sloane might pass right through her, too.

Seems ghosts are safer than people, Sloane thought.

"Maybe," she heard the echoing behind her now.

Sloane gasped. *Can you read my mind?*

"Maybe," the echo sounded again. Or was it the same maybe as before, still repeating itself in an otherwise echo-less house?

"Why are you here," Sloane asked aloud.

"Go outside," the ghost seemed to say.

Sloane felt her skin prickle. "What — why? I can't do that," she whispered.

"Go outside," it demanded.

"I guess I could try to check the mail," Sloane offered stiffly. She felt the hairs on her neck straighten and her heart start to race. She wondered if going outside was scarier than seeing ghosts in her house. She definitely needed a new therapist. For both agoraphobia *and* hallucinations.

"Do it now," the ghost whisper-yelled.

CHAPTER NINE

For whatever reason, knowing a ghost would scream at her if she didn't, Sloane suddenly felt like she needed to head outside. It would be the first time in a long time. She bolted downstairs and took deep, lengthy breaths as she grabbed the mail key and opened her door. She set her focus on the mailboxes directly in front of her house.

This will only take a few seconds, then I'll be back safely.

"Go outside," the voice echoed again, floating down the stairs like a ghoul.

Sloane didn't ask twice and dashed outside, shutting the ghost in the house. Out of the corner of her eye she saw a few neighbor's cars pull out of their driveways. Finally on their way to work, one by one they would slow near the yellow tape around Jackson's car and observe for a minute, as detectives and forensic inspectors took note of every last inch of the vehicle.

Sloane thought about Jackson and what might be happening to him right now. Was he being questioned? Was he behind bars? Did he murder his roommate?

She opened her mailbox and jostled a large stack out of the small unit. It had been a while since she'd had someone grab her mail. Even longer since she'd done it herself.

Her heart sped; she could feel it thumping in her chest. She peered back at her house but saw no movement. What Alanis's ghost still in there? Why was she supposed to go outside?

She took another deep breath and ventured a wider look around the neighborhood. The vantage point from here was much different than it was from her house.

Detectives stepped in and out of Jackson's house behind her, whispering and writing notes in their notepads. She saw Officer Byrd come out of Nina Smythe's townhouse, Nina right behind him, throwing her hands in the air and waving at the blight in her precious neighborhood. Byrd seemed eager to get away from her and continue his rounds, door to door, presumably asking people anything and everything about what they saw last night.

Most of the duplex townhouses were unbuilt or still empty, though, so doing rounds wouldn't take much longer for him. Sloane wondered if he'd opted for that job so that he wouldn't have to analyze a gory trunk all day.

There were only five completed duplexes in the neighborhood so far, and they weren't all lived in yet. A sixth, at the entrance to the neighborhood and just to the north of Sloane's duplex, was due for completion in a few months. The townhouse abutting Sloane's was still empty and, judging by Jose's puttering in there, still under construction.

She thought of Jose, who had bolted from the scene before the cops could question him.

She ventured a look at the unfinished units but saw no life. And no death, either. Alanis's ghost was nowhere.

Eventually, in a few years, the community would have twenty duplexes, 40 townhouses, so who knows how many neighbors? Sloane shivered and tried not to think about it. She checked that she had all the mail and scampered back to the safety of her townhouse.

When she'd bought the house, she'd liked the small development on rezoned farmland on the outskirts of town. It was two miles from the nearest traffic light, even more miles from big crowds. And, she'd believed, miles away from any dead people.

After berating Officer Byrd, Nina spotted Sloane and her mouth dropped open.

Sloane panicked and fidgeted with her door handle, hoping to beat it inside before Nina had a chance to yell at her about laundry. Out of the corner of her eye she thought she saw movement in the home attached to hers, but a second glance showed nothing. She sped into her house and locked the door three times behind her.

"Hello," she called up her stairs. There was no response.

She thought she felt a breeze from somewhere, but she couldn't immediately spot a source.

Had Alanis left?

She dared a peek through a small window near her stairs, which looked at the duplex across the alley, the Pacilli's house. The Smythes adjoined their duplex, but she couldn't see Nina from where her window was. She crouched on the stairs and thought of her neighbors.

In building next to the Smythe's, there was only the one resident, Principal Mackleby, who had moved in three or so weeks ago.

Across the road from Principal Mackleby, it appeared that strange large man had moved in, the one Sloane and Charlie had seen the other night. He had a new neighbor too, as Sloane frequently saw lights in the house at night. But Sloane didn't know who they were. She guessed it was someone who preferred to keep to themselves in the evening. She admired that.

Jackson was directly across the street from Sloane. Like Sloane's, his townhome didn't yet have a neighbor either. Theirs were the two newest buildings in the neighborhood, besides the unfinished shell.

The unfinished building at the entrance to the neighborhood was still a giant concoction of plywood and cement, and the townhouse abutting Sloane's was unfinished as well, but at least the siding was up. One day, the forest behind her would be torn down and a new street and houses would be built behind her, but there was no timeline for when. The houses weren't selling as fast as the builder had anticipated.

The community developers blamed the pandemic, but Sloane knew sales were slow due to the lack of available transit to the schools and center of the city. She had seen a few petitions circling the neighborhood requesting a decent bus route and more amenities, but for only 6 or 7 households lived in, it was going to be a tough sell to get anything built.

That's what Sloane liked about the neighborhood. Nobody and nothingness. The solitude.

Sloane's heart slowed and she padded upstairs to her main level, the echo of her own footsteps reverbing around her house. She wondered where Alanis' ghost had gone, and why it had wanted her outside.

Something felt off, and awkward. Sloane wondered if her mind was playing tricks on her.

Before venturing further into her house, she let her eyes roam from the living room through the kitchen and to the dining room. Everything was as it should be. So why did it feel so weird?

Then she spotted the balcony sheers slightly open.

"Alanis," she called. "Are you able to move the curtains?"

There was no response.

Sloane frowned. "I swear to god if that ghost can move things, I'm so screwed," she stomped over to the sheers and closed them, cocooning her house in a light-filled but closed-off space. "These stay closed, you hear me?" She called out to no one. The apparition was long gone.

Sloane frowned. "Why did she make me go outside?"

Sloane shrugged at herself. Since she'd been outside once already, she might as well do it again, this time behind the safety of her wrought-iron balcony railing. She picked up her laundry basket and took a deep breath, sliding open the balcony door through the sheers.

As she stepped outside, she felt a little more relaxed than she'd been in the past.

At nine o'clock, Construction workers started pulling into a sand lot behind the first building. A janky white Plymouth Reliant was permanently parked there, but otherwise the unfinished building had seemed cold and uninviting overnight. The workers pulled tools out of their trunks and headed into the building, bringing life with them.

Sloane folded a large bath towel. As she started a second fold, she saw Jose on the street. He walked behind the building and went to the Reliant, opened the trunk, and pulled out a construction helmet. A few construction workers walked over to talk to him, and they pointed and nodded towards the police tape.

Jose shook his head a few times and continued rifling through the trunk of his car, as some of the workers lit up cigarettes and chuckled about something.

Sloane wondered how they could be so carefree about a crime scene.

An officer at Jackson's house appeared to spot the small commotion, and he walked up the street toward the construction site. From her vantage point, Sloane could see a couple of workers dart away from the building toward the forest behind, Jose included. He moved so fast he'd neglected to shut the trunk of the Reliant.

She wondered what they were hiding. She hoped Jose was okay.

The wind caught Sloane's hair and she brushed it out of her eyes, a move the oncoming officer noticed from the street. His gaze lingered on her for a few seconds, and he looked back toward Jackson's car, as if to analyze her angle.

Sloane tensed. She'd already given two statements, and this was far too much exposure. She tried not to look back at the construction workers, hoping her distraction had given them a better chance to escape. At the same time, she couldn't stay outside any longer. This was too much exposure for one day.

Sloane dashed back inside, closing the door and the sheers behind her, escaping the outside world again.

CHAPTER TEN

An hour later, after Sloane had stressed-baked 30 sugar cookies, she eyed the remaining cop cars leaving the neighborhood. They must have finished collecting as much evidence as they could. She wondered if Jackson was home yet, or if he'd ever come home.

Sloane carefully placed twelve of the cookies in a small Christmas-themed cookie tin she'd found in a box. It recalled memories from a Christmas long past, with her ex. A time when she wasn't so afraid of everything.

She walked down to her foyer, ready to take a deep breath and open the front door, but a nagging feeling tugged at her senses.

Just behind her, the door of the empty bedroom was closed. She was certain she hadn't closed it. She never did.

A beam of light flickered from beneath the doorframe, and Sloane gasped. Was Alanis back?

Sloane braced herself, clutching the tin of cookies as though it were a protective shield. She twisted the doorknob and opened it slowly.

The room was empty, but the blinds were clacking in a light breeze. The window facing the backyard was slightly ajar. Sloane sighed. A cross breeze must have swung the room's door shut when went out to check the mail. She probably just didn't hear or see it when she rushed back inside.

She shifted the blinds to shut the pane, and she sucked in a breath. The screen was missing from the window.

"What the hell," she said to no one.

She took a breath and widened the window, just enough to stick her head out and look for the screen. She spotted it on the ground below. *How did that get there?* She wondered.

She closed the window and made a mental note to talk to Jose about the build quality of these windows. Nothing else in the room seemed amiss, so she told herself it was just a faulty screen.

Unfortunately, it's not like I can just pop outside and go get it.

She went back to the front door and opened it a crack. A cop car was pulling into the neighborhood. Her heart started beating faster, so she minimized the crack to barely the width of her pupil. She saw the car slow across the street. Jackson got out of the front seat, said something to the officer, nodded, and went into his house.

Sloane waited until the car had left before slowly widening the door. She checked to make sure there were no people wandering around the neighborhood. Out on the street, Jackson's car was still surrounded with yellow tape, but otherwise everyone seemed to be tucked away in their homes. There was no movement in Alanis' room at Jackson's townhouse, either. Sloane relaxed her shoulders, perhaps even the spirits were asleep, too.

To her right, the construction crew hammered at window installations from within the building on the corner, but they took no note of Sloane nor the street. Soft music could be heard via a boombox in the empty shell of a building.

Sloane stepped outside.

The air was brisk, and she wasn't sure if the hairs on her arm were bolt upright due to the chill of the weather, or her immense fear of outside. *It could be both.* She stepped carefully down the stairs, focusing on her feet alone. When her last foot left the bottom step of her property, she sped her pace and darted next door, reversing the motions up the stairs of the Pacilli's house. Ringing their doorbell, she held her breath. She was still outside, but she felt safer being next to a building, even if it wasn't hers.

From right next door, Nina Smythe opened her own door and poked her head out. Sloane tensed but smiled at her, then knocked rapidly on Francesca's door. She heard the soft padding of the pregnant woman descending the stairs. Nina scowled, then retreated back into her house. Sloane felt herself relax. Thank goodness the nosy woman hadn't tried to talk to her.

Francesca appeared genuinely confused when she opened the door, smiling at Sloane, but looking out over her shoulder to double-check on that morning's drama. Once she'd seen that the cars and police officer weren't there, her shoulders crept down from her ears, and she smiled at Sloane.

"Hello," Francesca said in a thick accent.

"Hello," Sloane stuttered, then she remembered why she was there. "I baked you some cookies." Like an afterthought, she added, "As a sort of baby shower gift."

Francesca stared at her, not understanding.

Sloane brought out the tin out from its position against her chest and opened it up so Francesca could see. The little sugar cookies were in various shapes - a crawling baby, a baby bottle, a toy.

"Cookies," Francesca squealed, sounding almost like a little baby herself. "Grazie."

"You're welcome," Sloane breathed. A bead of sweat formed on her temple. The world behind her was creeping over her shoulder like something out of a horror movie.

Francesca smiled, cradling the cookie tin on her protruding belly.

Sensing that they had nothing further to discuss, Sloane backed away slowly towards the steps and street. As Francesca closed the door behind her, Sloane sprinted the rest of the way to her front door, her eyes nearly closed into slits, her hands hiding her face like horse blinders. She didn't want to *see*.

"Jackson!" She heard Jackson yell from across the road. She'd barely got her hand on her doorknob. Sweat dripped rolled down her forehead and her heartbeat quickened.

Breathe, she told herself, just breathe.

"Sloane," again Jackson spoke, closer to her this time, having crossed the road in a split second.

Sloane's brain went fuzzy. She turned the knob of her house and took a step inside, which calmed her enough to turn and face him on the porch.

"Jackson," she said slowly, "more mail?" She'd been so tense about being outside, she'd almost completely forgot about this morning's experience with Alanis, and that Jackson was probably dealing with much more significant things than misplaced mail. When she remembered, she shook her head and plastered a sympathetic smile across her face. "How are you? I'm so sorry."

Jackson looked toward where his car used to be, and his shoulders slumped. He smiled at Sloane for a moment, and for a brief second she wondered if he was worried, or maybe guilty.

"It's-" he began, "It was complicated. Alanis was my cousin but she and I weren't super cl-"

He stopped himself and didn't continue that thought. "I don't have mail for you. I just wanted to see someone familiar. I'm sorry. I won't bother you."

Sloane relaxed a little. She wasn't sure what the best thing to say was, but it certainly wasn't humor, she thought immediately after her mouth said, "Coppers let you off early, huh? Good behavior?"

She mentally kicked herself. She had no idea what he had been through.

Jackson's shoulders appeared to tense, but he smiled. "I'm not supposed to leave town. I think I can go to work and back home, and that's it."

"You don't have to tell me anything," Sloane offered. "You're not on trial with me. I read enough of your mail to know you used to subscribe to the cheese of the month club."

At this, Jackson laughed. "Thanks."

Out of the corner of her eye, Sloane saw Nina Smythe exit her house and look up and down the street. When she spotted the two of them, she kept her eyes on Jackson.

Sloane took a step back into her house and stepped slightly behind her door, a move that Jackson seemed to take as a rejection. He took a step backwards toward the front steps. It didn't appear that he'd noticed Nina.

Sloane felt bad, he must have thought she was afraid of him. She tried to open the door a little wider to be more welcoming, but the cold air began to overwhelm her. "If you need anything at all, do come by. I just dropped some cookies off at Francesca's house, and I have some more upstairs."

At this, Jackson looked toward the Pacilli's house and spotted Nina on the street, both hands on her hips. He nodded to Nina, turned back toward Sloane, and discreetly rolled his eyes. "Thanks," he said, and withdrew back toward his house.

Sloane slammed her door a little loudly and locked it, hoping Nina wasn't planning to come yell at her about laundry. The experience of taking cookies next door and having extra sets of eyes on her was already too much for one day.

She raced up her staircase and right into the plasma of Alanis's ghost.

CHAPTER ELEVEN

"Fucking hell," Sloane yelled, shuddering and shaking her body as though ghost entrails were stuck to it. Alanis hovered near the top of the staircase, staring out a window toward the duplex next door. The apparition did not appear to give a shit that Sloane had just busted through it at top speed.

"She's coming," Alanis's voice echoed.

"Who is coming?" Sloane brushed her shirt with her hands, as though still trying to dispose of the ghost like it was cat hair. She knew she looked ridiculous. She knew there was nothing there. But it *felt* like something was there. She checked her backside.

She was already terribly weirded out, so the loud knock at the door made her jump ten feet out of her body.

"Who is here? Nina? What the hell could she want from me?" she asked Alanis's ghost.

But the ghost had already half-evaporated. It turned and looked her dead in the eye as it whispered, "She is here."

Sloane watched the ghost disappear. She didn't bother asking again. Instead, she crept downstairs to return to the front door.

She hoped it was Francesca coming to thank her for the cookies. Maybe it was the woman cop from early this morning, telling her to back off from her sexy coworker Drew Byrd.

Sloane laughed at herself. She had zero interested in police officers.

She wondered if it was Charlie, visiting after a morning at her massage studio, maybe bringing another bottle of wine.

Perhaps it was another dead body.

Sloane shuddered.

Or maybe the ghost didn't know genders, and it was Jackson. Maybe he'd forgotten to give her some mail or tell her why he killed Alanis.

She felt immediate shame at the thought, wanting instead to believe her handsome neighbor was innocent. He's got to be, she told herself. But considering Occam's razor, she wasn't entirely sure she wasn't kidding herself.

A very decent part of her felt he was innocent. She laughed at herself and inched open the door.

It was Nina. The permanently frowning eyebrows gave her away instantly.

Nina huffed, "Sorry to bother you, Sloane." Her timbre made it sound more like *Sloane* was bothering *her*.

Sloane focused on her breathing for a split second, then took a careful step onto the threshold, looking out over Nina's shoulder for people, or spirits, or dead bodies.

She returned her attention to the neighbor and smiled. "No problem, Nina. I wasn't expecting you."

"What did Jackson say to you? Is he under house arrest?"

Sloane kept the smile plastered on her face and resisted rolling her eyes. She would not give into whatever gossip Nina had in mind. The woman would have to attack someone else for a story.

Sloane responded with, "I don't think so." Then, to try and offer a reason, even though she felt Nina didn't need one, she lied. "We were just exchanging mail again."

Why did *he come over*, the thought occurred to her.

"Oh, I see." Nina looked across the road to Jackson's front door. "Do you think he's guilty?"

"Guilty of being cool? Sure," snarked Sloane. "But I don't think he had anything to do with this." She almost waved her hand behind her as though Alanis's body were still floating in her kitchen, but quickly put it away when she realized how ridiculous that would look. Instead, as she began to close the door, she asked, "Was there anything else you wanted?"

Nina was having none of it, angling a foot almost directly into the door jamb. "Will you be at the Homeowner's meeting on Thursday? It's our first one since we formed our private group. It's at my house. I'm president!"

"I don't think so," said Sloane. No, she definitely would *not* be attending any HOA meeting, even if it were in her own home and away from people. She especially was not interested in a meeting where Nina Smythe had declared herself president of a group no one else seemed to care about.

"Think about it! I know you take issue with some of the stuff going on in the neighborhood. Maybe that could be a line item on our agenda! Maybe you could be the Vice President of Outside Decorations!"

Sloane stared at her for a good three seconds in sheer disbelief, her bottom lip aching from her teeth gnawing into it. She blinked twice and responded, "I guess I'll see." She looked back over her own shoulder, almost hoping a ghost would pop out and scare Nina away. Instead, she lied, "I have to go, I have cookies baking."

As she went to shut the door in her unwelcome guest's face, Nina said "Great! Think about it. Also, bring those cookies to share!"

Sloane mumbled a goodbye and closed the door. She glared at the back of it for a few seconds, trying to figure out what her next move was, while also listening for Nina's footsteps to retreat. There was no point engaging in a homeowner's meeting when she had only recently moved in. Then again, most of the neighbors had only recently moved in. As she stood in her foyer staring at nothing, Sloane gave it more thought. The meeting might include some new introductions, something Sloane might need if she wanted to figure out if there was a killer in the neighborhood. The Smythe's townhouse was only in the next duplex, just a tiny bit further than Francesca's door. It would be like going to the mailbox and back.

She shook her head at herself as she padded around the foyer. She wasn't a detective or private investigator and, suffering with agoraphobia, no one was going to make her chief intelligence officer for the feds anytime soon, either.

As she paced by the first-floor bedroom, she peeked inside it, noting the empty white walls and vacant space. She hadn't bothered to paint when she moved in, knowing she'd never have a use for the room given that she hated being on ground level. Someday, maybe she'd get over her fear of the front door and everyone on the other side of it. But that someday was *not* today.

She walked through the vacant room and peered out the back window, making sure the screen was still on the ground below. She dared to look a little further out, toward the back fence and the forest. The cluster of trees added comfort to her cocoon, and stretched for several acres toward the city. A gate in the back fence led to a small, shared neighborhood path between the forest and her fence. It would be perfect for runners or pet owners, if any were to move into her neighborhood. She wondered if the path met up with the other end of the street, where the large man with the small dog had just moved in.

She imagined it did but didn't dare walk outside to check it out. She'd never seen the man behind her house at all. Granted, she hardly looked outside.

A dark spot by her back fence caught her attention, the smallest of idiosyncrasies in her new manicured lawn next to the wild woods. A dark purple spot, not much larger than a sock, but unusually colored enough that the sun, now breaking through the gray clouds, caught it in the light.

As though biologically instinctual, Sloane knew it was dried blood. She ran upstairs to find her cellphone to call detective Drew Byrd.

CHAPTER TWELVE

Alanis's ghost was back, hovering by the balcony window.

"What is all of this about, lady?" Sloane was too frustrated and frightened to care about apparitions appearing and disappearing anymore. She jumped right into condemnation.

The ghost seemed to watch her old house across the street. "I don't know," the apparition said.

Sloane paused, her anger fading. She stood by her kitchen island and tried to think about what to say. "Who were you, Alanis?"

"Alive," the ghost's voice echoed around Sloane's dining room.

\#

Sloane did her best to get as much information out of Alanis as she could, but the apparition did not seem to know anything about how she'd died. The conversation, if that's what it could be considered, stayed light, and echoey, and not at all revealing about who might have wanted Alanis dead.

"He's here," Alanis finally whispered, disappearing into nothingness.

A knock sounded at the door, and Sloane didn't resist climbing down the stairs and opening it this time. Whatever Alanis' spirit was doing in her house, it didn't mean her any harm, and it seemed to know when Sloane could avoid harm, too.

Dressed in a flannel shirt that almost burst at the bulk of his biceps, Drew Byrd stepped inside without asking, once Sloane had fully opened the door for him.

"That didn't take long," Sloane said, although she actually wasn't quite sure how long she'd been chatting with Alanis.

"I'm always in the neighborhood," he winked.

She felt a flutter in her belly. Was he flirting with her? Instinctually, her eyes dropped to his left hand, then she shook her head at herself. Although harmless flirting with a handsome cop never hurt anyone, she did *not* have the mental space for it.

Sloane smiled up to him, trying to avoid gawking at his fit shoulders.

His face mirrored her smile, but then grew serious. "You said you spotted something in your back yard? I've already notified the department, so they're sending another investigator over here now. Why don't you take me back there and show me what you saw."

Sloane froze, the skin on her arm forming tiny goosebumps. Could she walk out back? Even with the security of a handsome police officer beside her? She took a tentative step forward, toward the front step, and her heart began to race.

"I actually can't leave the house right now," she croaked. How could she easily explain this away? "I have an operation running on my computer upstairs," she lied. "I need to listen for it to, uh, finish."

What the hell bullshit computational lies are you spreading, she berated herself.

Drew raised an eyebrow.

"Can you just come in and look at it from here?" She stood back and waved him inside.

He clomped in and looked down at his boots.

"It's fine," she said. She waved him toward the back room and followed behind as he headed toward the window.

Drew walked through the empty bedroom. If its blankness seemed odd to him, he didn't say anything. When he saw the screenless window, he asked, "What happened here?"

"I think it was the wind or something. The screen is on the ground."

Drew knit his eyebrows together. "You have to secure this, what with a potential killer wandering around the neighborhood. I wouldn't want you to be next."

Sloane tried to ignore the threat, instead daring a look outside.

She felt the officer's hand on her lower back, as he leaned over her shoulder to look at where she was pointing. She loved how warm his grasp was. Drew spotted the blood and grabbed his phone out of his pocket, removing his hand from Sloane's lower back. She frowned.

He snapped a picture from her vantage point, then headed back toward the front door. Sloane followed.

"If it's all the same to you, Officer -"

"Drew's fine."

"-if you don't need me, I'll go back upstairs."

For a split second, his gaze lingered on her as though he were trying to puzzle her out. She closed her eyes and held the doorframe to steady herself, then opened them again when she no longer felt like she was falling. Her lower back shook, longing for a comforting hand again.

She saw a police car enter the neighborhood, and Drew waved it down. He turned and nodded at her again, and when the car stopped and the officers got out, the three of them walked back through the alleyway between Sloane's and the Pacilli's house. She closed her door and relaxed her breath.

Sloane snuck back to the empty bedroom and watched them approach the bloodstain.

She cracked open the window a bit so she could hear what they were saying. She thought she'd been quiet enough, but Drew heard the sound and turned to face her window.

"Hey Sloane," he called. "Please stick around in case my colleagues want to talk to you."

Sloane nodded, then slammed the window shut.

A few deep breaths later, and she was back to her usual tense-but-comfortable level. She walked back upstairs and chose instead to watch the events unfold from her living room window, at the back of her house but on a level higher up than the ground. Somehow, she felt less exposed being further away.

A few times, Drew looked up to see if he could spot her in the downstairs window, but it took him a minute to see her in the living room. She waved at him from there, and he smiled at her.

Then, his eye seemed to catch a distraction, either behind the Pacilli's townhouse or near the alley he'd just walked through. He gestured to it and the inspector and forensics expert followed his finger to another spot in the dirt.

More blood?

The investigator turned toward Sloane's house and yelled something. She stepped back and a fourth person, a female officer, walked out from the alley, startling her. The woman pulled out a roll of yellow tape and began attaching it to the back of Sloane's house. Sloane took this as her cue to leave. This was too much to watch in real life. If she wanted CSI and a murder mystery, she had a TV. She ran all the way upstairs and hid in her windowless master bathroom. It was all too much.

CHAPTER THIRTEEN

"Woman!" Charlie screamed from the front door, shutting it behind her and bounding up the stairs. Sloane was in the middle of removing a fresh set of chocolate chip cookies from the oven. Although she'd heard the door open, she didn't panic this time. A surprisingly nice step toward progress, she thought. She did feel her body ease at hearing Charlie's voice, however, so she had experienced at least some level of anxiety.

She took a quick glance around her main floor, to make sure any ghosts were not around. *Although I probably just imagined Alanis before*, she thought to herself, curling her lip. *I might need to start antipsychotics.*

"Hey babe," she turned her frown into a smile and acknowledged Charlie as she reached the top of the stairs.

A look of anger and excitement flowed over Charlie's face. "You had a murder here yesterday and you didn't call me? What is wrong with you? It's all over the news that some hot woman was found in the trunk of a car! Did you think I wouldn't panic?"

"The news said she was 'hot?'"

"I surmised it, asshole. Dead women are always hot."

"I didn't even think about the news," Sloane bit her lip. She hadn't. How many other people in her life might wonder if she was alright? She'd been so busy thinking about how this all affected her anxiety, she'd forgotten that other humans might care about her welfare, too.

Then, she remembered that the only people she had in her extremely small circle were Charlie, her old friends and family who had chosen Brian in the divorce, or a dead person casually floating in and out of her house.

Not having friends was the sad reality when one had trouble leaving their house. Charlie was her last remaining living guest.

Sloane put the tray of cookies down and walked around the island with her arms open for a hug. "I'm sorry."

Charlie held the hug for an unusually long time. "Don't scare me like that. You need to text me any time something happens."

"You know that it wouldn't have been me, right? I can barely leave my house and I don't know anybody. How am I going to end up in the trunk of someone's car?"

Charlie dove for the baking tray, winced at the heat on her fingers, and tossed a small, soft cookie between her hands to cool it off. "Whose cars are out front? Are the detectives still here?"

"They're out back, come see." Sloan guided her over to the living room window. "That's Drew, the officer who I met the other day," she said.

"Oh! Drew Byrd? I know him. He's dreamy!"

"How do you know him?"

"We've worked with him out at our little bar. Darius wanted to get to know all the local cops, for his own safety. Officer Byrd is a total cutie."

"He's definitely not bad on the eyes," agreed Sloane. "But he has the outline of a ring on his finger."

"Uh-uh," Charlie shook her head, mumbling with half a cookie in her mouth. "I know he's not married. I asked him about it last time he checked in at the bar."

"Why'd you do that?"

"For you, birdbrain. You have to get out there into the dating pool. Speaking of relationships, have you heard from Brian?"

"No, why would I?" Sloane backed away from the window and retreated to the kitchen to move the hot cookies from the tray to a cooling rack.

"Don't you think he'd be worried?"

"I don't know. Maybe he'd be glad. He could get his deck chairs back," Sloane winked. Charlie frowned at her. "Plus, he's far enough away that small town Jefferson City news probably hasn't reached him in Chicago."

"Don't be silly. You should call him."

"I'll send him a text." She grabbed her cellphone off the counter and sent a quick note:

> Sloane: Did not bite the big one,
>   unless we're referencing my
>   chocolate chip cookies.
>   Didn't want you to worry.

She stared at her phone for a second, wondering if he'd respond right away. When she looked up again, Charlie was already by the fridge holding a bottle of Reisling and two glasses. She nodded toward the balcony. "Care to test your comfort levels, babe?"

Sloane's phone buzzed back.

> Brian: I do miss your cookies.
>   ...and your baked goods, too!
>   ;) Stay alive, thanks.

Sloane smiled at the message. He was always cracking sexy puns, and obviously had not stopped even though the marriage had dissolved. She felt comforted to know she still had him in her life, even if her agoraphobia had split them apart. His message warmed her heart enough to step out on the balcony without caution.

Charlie raised an eyebrow at her, but Sloane rolled her eyes. "It's not like that."

"You still like him," Charlie teased, opening the balcony door.

Sloane hummed in the negative, but her heart did hurt a little. Maybe being alone wasn't all it was cracked up to be.

The women sat sipping their wines, and Sloane described the entire day, leaving out the descriptive and sordid displeasure that was Alanis's mangled body, and the odd experience of chatting with a ghost.

As they talked, Leonardo pulled his car up to the front of the house and waved up at them, before looking back toward where Jackson's black sedan had sat during the hubbub this morning. Francesca waddled out onto their porch and started worriedly saying things in Italian, pointing at the police officers' vehicles. Sloane remembered that Leonardo had left before the detectives had begun their rounds of the neighborhood, and Francesca probably couldn't answer many of their questions. Leonardo said something back to her and then dipped into the alley between the buildings, presumably to find Drew or one of the other officers.

Nina also came out on her porch, but when she spotted Francesca, her face seemed to turn sour. She shrugged, then occupied herself watering her potted plants.

Charlie nodded toward Nina and muttered under her breath, "She's kind of a busybody, that one. Isn't she?"

Sloane smiled, but felt sympathetic, and a little guilty for being a gossip. "I presume she's just bored during the day while her husband works."

"Still, girl needs a hobby."

"She has declared herself president of the Homeowner's Association. She's having a meeting at her house on Thursday."

"Are you going?" Charlie asked this mockingly, and Sloane chuckled.

"Oh yes, I'll pack some cookies and we'll talk about festive holiday decorations. It will be a grand time!" Sloane's sarcastic response invoked a loud guffaw out of Charlie, and Nina turned her head to see them. They both waved at her, feeling sheepish.

Nina descended from her porch, passed widely in front of the Pacilli's house, then peered through the alleyway as though looking to see where Leonardo had gone. Then she called up to the women. "Sloane, what are the police doing in your backyard?"

"Oh, you noticed them? That's where she stores her sexy officers," Charlie chuckled at herself and elbowed Sloane.

Nina frowned. "Seriously, what is happening in your yard?"

"They're looking for evidence to indict me," joked Sloane.

"They'll never catch you alive!" Charlie added.

Nina scowled. "Please. We all know who really did it." She rolled her eyes and angled her head toward Jackson's house behind her.

Sloane grew angry, clenching her fists. Charlie put a hand on her arm to soothe her. "Let it go," she whispered.

Sloane broke into a light smile. She was *not* going to engage with the neighborhood snoop today.

Nina changed topics. "You're coming to my meeting Thursday, right?"

"I don't know," said Sloane, desperately trying to come up with an excuse. But what sort of excuse could a woman who never leaves her house have? Failing to come up with any valid reason why she couldn't walk the two houses over, she added "I'll see."

This appeared good enough for Nina, and she wished them a good day, returning to her house. She didn't even pretend to finish watering her plants.

Sloane's skin prickled, and her hands clenched the armrests of her camping chair.

Charlie sipped her wine. "Do you want me to come?"

"Where? Nina's house? You'd hate it."

"True, but your mental health is more important to me than dying of HOA boredom."

"We'll see, but yes I'd love it if you'd come over on Thursday." Having a friend to walk with her might ease Sloane's journey next door but, as with any time she had to leave the house, she'd have to go by how she felt.

"I'm not working Thursday anyway. Appointments are slow at the massage studio, and I took the Sunday brunch shift at the bar instead of Thursday nights. There are better tips."

Conversation was lighter after that, although they still shared a fair amount of back and forth over who murdered Alanis. Sloane worried about saying too much, but Charlie didn't seem to notice that Sloane knew or cared about Alanis more than she had the last time Charlie visited.

CHAPTER FOURTEEN

An hour after Charlie left, after wrangling with the laundry machine and microwaving herself a TV dinner (organic, so she felt a little better about her poor eating habits), Sloane heard a light knock at the door.

She guessed that it might be Drew, telling her they had finished up in the back, so she was not nervous about bounding down the stairs and opening the door. That is until she did so.

She started speaking as she opened the door, saying, "Are you guys all done?" but her face fell a bit upon seeing Jackson. She stopped herself and attempted to perk up. At least it wasn't Nina again.

Jackson held his left hand on the door frame and ran his right hand through his hair, nervously. He offered a smile and said, "They are done, yes, but I wouldn't classify myself as one of *them*." He lengthened the last word in stark condemnation.

Sloane smiled at him. She peered over his shoulder and noticed that the police cars and Drew's car had left the scene already, then she looked back at her guest. "Have more mail for me?"

He shuffled his feet a bit, removed his left hand from the doorframe and rubbed his hands together. "No, uh, no. Actually, I wondered if you--" he paused, as though looking for a word.

Sloane felt herself devolving into sympathy. Clearly, Jackson had suffered a much longer, much worse day than she'd had. But if he was a killer--like Nina, Drew, and probably the whole neighborhood seemed to think he was--she was defenseless.

If she was going to die, she decided at that moment to be nice about it. "Why don't you come in?" She opened the door and offered him space.

"Are you sure?" Jackson looked out over his shoulder, eyeing the neighborhood.

Making sure there are no witnesses?

Sloane regretted the thought.

She nodded, "You've had a long day and I have cookies and wine. It's win-win."

He muttered thanks and came into the house. She shut the door and triple-bolted it behind him. He watched her with raised eyebrows. "What's up with your three bolts? Should I be concerned about my safety?"

"I'm sorry," she tried to feign a laugh. "It's a long story." It wasn't, but his situation was far more interesting than her mental illness, so she didn't want to talk about herself.

As they turned toward the stairs, Jackson eyed the empty downstairs room in the back, as though analyzing it for something. Then he admired the fresh blue paint on the staircase leading into bright red in the kitchen. Sloane was proud of her decorative choices, a comforting cocoon of warmth in what was her permanent mental prison.

"This is the mirror image of my house," Jackson offered as conversation, "Although your bedroom downstairs faces a different way, and of course your bold color choices are different."

"What color did you paint yours?"

"It's still the boring apartment-white they sold the houses with. I'm not creative enough to come up with a color scheme. Alanis's room is, was, uh--" he briefly lost his train of thought.

He continued, "She'd hung bright purple art, but that was about it."

"She had the downstairs room?" Sloane looked around the main floor for Alanis's ghost, but it wasn't there. Sloane knew that it had been her room and that she'd decorated it, both from seeing Alanis in the window and later talking to her ghost, but she didn't want to give any of her background knowledge away to Jackson. She certainly didn't want him to know that she could have two-way conversations with the dead.

"Yes," he sighed. Sloane had almost forgotten what she'd asked him.

She walked around the island to the fridge and grabbed an open bottle of white, the bottle Charlie and she hadn't finished. She held it up for his approval, and he nodded. She considered asking him if he'd like to talk about how it went at the police station, or if he maybe wanted to speak about Alanis, or something else. Any question she could come up with seemed gossipy and demanding.

Instead, she offered a weak smile and a glass of wine. "Do you want to sit in here, or out on the balcony?"

"Living room, if you don't mind. The neighbors are all up in my business."

"I know the feeling," she said before thinking, then reprimanded herself for once again being too self-involved to realize that he was hurting a million times worse than she was.

"The truth about Alanis is that I barely knew her," Jackson finally said, after they'd sat and sipped their wine for a minute. Sloane stayed silent and let him continue. As long as she didn't ask the leading questions, she wouldn't consider herself a busybody. Jackson continued, "We were related, I guess my dad and her dad were cousins or whatever, but we weren't buddy-buddy or anything. When I heard through the grapevine that she needed a room after rehab, I offered her the first floor for a low price. Some cash is always nice, you know?" He didn't wait for an answer. His voice softened and he repeated again, "I barely knew her. She came and went as she chose. She didn't drive, but

she seemed to like taking walks around the neighborhood and--
" Jackson's lip quivered.

Sloane waited for a beat, then she couldn't resist. She had to ask a pressing question, "So, what happened?"

Jackson perked up and his eyes grew wide. "Well, I didn't kill her, if that's what you're ask-!"

Sloane interjected, "I never thought you did!" It was a bald-faced lie, and she kicked herself for doubting him, but at the same time she couldn't be honest when he was sitting right there in her living room.

Truth was, like Drew and Nina and everyone else in the neighborhood, she too had occasionally experienced doubt. The simplest answer was usually the truth, right? Now, looking at him sitting in the raw light, helpless in her living room, that prior doubt was dissolving. He was genuinely upset.

Jackson laughed, nervously. "I just don't know what to do. The cops don't want me to go far, just to work and back, so I guess I have to stick around, but this neighborhood and these neighbors-" he trailed off again and looked into the distance, as though peering out through the walls.

"Forget the neighbors," Sloane scoffed, and fluffed her hand toward the nothingness Jackson stared at. "Let them think what they think for now. The truth will come out."

"What truth, though? What truth?" Jackson shook his hair out with one hand, completely defeated.

Sloane eyed his wine glass; he'd barely imbibed a drop. Her glass, however, was already empty. She rose from the couch to go get the dregs of the wine bottle from the kitchen. "What about Alanis's family? Or friends?"

"Nothing there. My dad's cousin lives in another state, and Alanis's friends were at some concert or something."

"Convenient alibis! *Too* convenient." Sloane smirked.

At this, Jackson laughed. He rose from his seat and followed Sloane into the kitchen, keeping a cautious distance. She wanted to make him feel comfortable in her space. She believed him, so she closed the gap and gave him an awkward but friendly hug.

His arms were strong and warm, but stiff, and his hug was careful and protected. He smelled of Old Spice and longing.

She backed off quickly. "I know it's hard for you right now, but you're always welcome to visit me any time."

"Thanks, Sloane." Jackson softened his stoic position, then his face brightened. "Can I take you out for dinner?"

"No!" Sloane said, too quickly.

"Woah, sorry. I didn't mean like a date or anything," Jackson was backpedaling, "I just meant-" his eyes darted toward her microwaveable meal.

"I'm sorry Jackson, I can't. I can't go out."

"Oh? I see."

"But why don't you come over for dinner tomorrow night? We can order Chinese and watch a movie or something."

Jackson twisted his eyebrows in confusion. Being rejected but then immediately asked out again must have seemed weird to him, Sloane supposed, but he didn't need to know her psychosomatic issues just now. He had other things to worry about.

She looked around for Alanis's ghost. Still not there.

Jackson nodded his agreement and retreated toward the staircase down to the door.

Downstairs, as Sloane unbolted her prison vault, Jackson looked back at the empty white room and sighed. Sloane wondered if he was thinking about Alanis. She put her hand on his shoulder as she opened the door, only checking briefly for the threat of the outside world. He tapped her hand with his and thanked her again.

Having one friend in the neighborhood would help Jackson relax, and it might also help Sloane out with her problems down the line, too.

She just didn't know how much, yet.

CHAPTER FIFTEEN

Sloane slept in the next day, waking up briefly when the sounds of the Pacilli's arguing carried up through the alley again. She passed out again shortly thereafter. The previous day's events were more intense, and the visitors more abundant, than she'd experienced in the last several years.

At nine, her eyes popped open again, and she spotted the ghost of Alanis hanging out by the master bedroom window. Sloane felt eerily calm about it. She remained snuggled in bed, flipping back and forth in semi slumber, lucidly dreaming about neighbors and police officers and ghosts and friends.

She finally awoke at ten, Alanis was still floating languidly by the window.

"Everything alright?" Sloane asked the apparition.

"Alright," Alanis confirmed.

Sloane crawled out of her bed, her muscles creaking from oversleeping. "Sometimes I don't know if you're echoing me, or talking to me," Sloane muttered.

"Talking," the apparition voiced.

"Exactly, see? What was that?" Sloane walked into her bathroom to prep for a shower. She realized closing the door was futile, as it was possible Alanis could just wander around freely through the walls, but she did so anyway. Might as well get the most privacy she could.

"I'm dead," Alanis said. "But I'm talking." The apparition began to disappear.

"Fair enough," Sloane replied, shutting the door. To the closed doorframe, she whispered, "Then why won't you tell me how you died?"

Everything about her body was sore and exhausted, and both the shower and the coffee machine seemed to take longer than normal. But that first inhale of smoky hazelnut roasted bean melted into her senses like chocolate. She could make a day of nothing but coffee for breakfast, lunch, and dinner.

Dinner. Sloane suddenly remembered she'd invited Jackson over for dinner. This thought took her into the dining area to the balcony window. Would the neighborhood be quiet, post murder? Would Nina still be gawking and postulating and supposing? Would Francesca and Leonardo argue or wish each other well on the front porch?

Sloane peered through the sheer curtains and saw no one, so she deemed it safe to step out onto the balcony.

She looked backwards into her house, but Alanis had not reappeared since their interaction earlier.

Her steps were tentative. Without Charlie to lead the way, she was fully exposed to the outside world. She opened the door three quarters of the way and squeezed through, as though the house was birthing her out onto her balcony. She paused, and held the door behind her, leaning against it so as to grab on for dear life. Her coffee steamed in the chilly air, and she admired the whorls of smoke swirling in the gentle breeze. Careless, free.

A movement down the road caught her eye. Principal Mackleby walked out of Nina Smythe's house and down her front steps. She stood in the road for a moment, adjusted her pantsuit and pulled down her jacket, and then got into her red car a few yards away. She didn't notice Sloane.

Interesting, thought Sloane, Nina and Ken didn't have kids, so Mackleby might have been there discussing HOA issues.

Unless they were doing something untoward. Afternoon Delight on a school day? Tsk tsk, you two vixens.

Sloane smiled at her wild imagination, but attempted not to move until the car was out of sight, lest she catch the woman's attention. That would be too much for her.

Nina emerged from her house not a few seconds later, and after scanning all the townhouses like a periscope, her eyes alighted on Sloane. She waved and smiled but pulled her hand back quickly. She seemed to stare nervously into her planter boxes.

Sloane gulped and tried to avoid looking at her.

To Sloane's right, the newest neighbor, the man with the dog who lived up the street, came out from around the plyboard walls of the undeveloped first building. He had his hands shoved deep into his pockets, and his tiny dog followed behind him on a loose lead. His face aimed pointedly at the ground, and he marched quickly past Jackson's duplex and toward his own house.

Nina spotted him and squealed "Rick!"

The man froze, looked from side to side like he'd been caught at something, then gave Nina a curt and pleasant nod. He sped his gait up a bit, and the small dog huffed to catch up.

Rick? Jose had said his name was Ricardo, but Sloane supposed that was the same thing. She promised herself she would never think of him as the strange dog-walking guy ever again. She slipped down into one of her balcony seats, soundlessly.

Nina didn't appear to notice Rick's rejection of her at all. She called to the man, "You're coming to the meeting Thursday, right? I'll have hors d'oevres."

Rick continued walking. He looked at his watch as though it would give him an excuse and said, "I don't know."

Nina continued, "Sloane might bring cookies!" She gestured her hand up toward where Sloane was sitting.

Sloane's spine bolted straight. She didn't need nor want introductions to strangers right then. Behind her buttocks the chilly director's chair had grown warm, but with the shift in position she'd felt a breeze blow behind her, making the shivers in her body even worse than usual. She froze, terrified.

Rick spun around and looked up at Sloane's balcony. He seemed nervous as well, clearly surprised she'd been there all along. Both Sloane and Rick tried to ease their deer-in-the-headlights posture and gave each other a nervous wave.

Rick turned and ran into his house. Sloane stood and escaped into her own. To Nina, it must have been a bizarre show, and Sloane wondered if he had a psychological trauma of his own. Simple introversion? A fear of being discovered for murder? Or merely discomfort at being spoken to when he's just trying to walk his dog? It would be a fully understandable condition, in Sloane's opinion.

Sloane closed the sliding glass door, the frightening sounds of everyday existence whooshing out of the vacuum of her house. She stared into her empty kitchen, letting her gaze drift through to the empty living room, all the way out through the curtains at the back of the house, and into the dark forest. Was she safe here? Would she be able to carry on living when the very thought of existing outside her cocoon gave her heart palpitations and a panic attack?

She thought of Alanis, the once-living Alanis, and how she was merely trying to get straight and restart her life. She maybe have been troubled once, sure. But she most definitely did not intend to die and be shoved in a trunk. Sloane was dealing with her own issues, but she herself had nowhere to go. Would she also die, alone and cold at night? Who would find her?

Charlotte. Charlie would find her, eventually. She'd come bouncing in, after a slow afternoon at the massage parlor, or a night dealing with difficult drinkers at the pub. She'd bound in with a smile on her face and find Sloane's mangled body, probably in bed where she spent most of her time.

Someone near to Sloane's location was a murderer, possibly a murderer of single women, and Sloane was one of the last remaining single women around.

She called Charlie and left a voice message. "Can you come stay with me for a bit? I don't want to be alone."

CHAPTER SIXTEEN

It turned out Charlie was eager to visit. Now that she was in a permanent relationship with her handsome pub co-owner Darius, she wanted to ceremoniously delete her Dateme.com profile, and she needed Sloane's company to do it.

"I'm not sure Darius is the right person to do this with," Charlie laughed. "He's been upset that I still get daily pings from random men!"

The two of them sat out on the balcony, Sloane much more comfortable outside when Charlie was around. Charlie let her do the honors with her dating app.

Charlie's DateMe profile pic showed her adorable braids and her hugging a bottle of Heineken. Her dark brown eyes looked mischievously off toward the right, and her mouth was in a wide smile with her tongue licking toward the bottle. Sloane didn't understand it at all.

"I get over 100 pings a day," Charlie gushed, pointing out cute guys who have sent her messages.

Sloane furrowed her nose and scoffed.

Charlie caught her stare. "You could do it too, you know. I could make a profile for you."

Before Sloane could protest, Charlie had grabbed her phone back and was already creating a new DateMe profile, listing Sloane as a "homebody" who loved to "cook meals and stay inside cuddling."

"That's a nice way of saying that I can't leave my house," said Sloane.

"You have to be honest without scaring the crap out of people!" laughed Charlie. "Guys don't want to hear that you're a divorced miser with an anxiety disorder, they want to hear that you're a cuddly baker with a passion for Netflix and Chillin'.''

Sloane shook her head. Principal Mackleby's car turned down the street, slowing has she looked up at the women on Sloane's balcony. She waved at them, and Sloane nodded.

"New gal pal?" Charlie said over her shoulder.

"No, I don't know anything about her. Plus, I think she might be doing it with Nina."

"What?! I must know more."

Sloane backpedaled. "I'm kidding. I saw her come out of her house yesterday, they might have been prepping for the HOA meeting tomorrow, I don't know. Nina probably made her Deputy of Single Residents or something like that."

"That could be your job. Are you going?"

"What? No. Nina wants to make me décor cop or something. Like I'm supposed to hand out violation sanctions to anyone who hangs their laundry on the balcony. It's a way to get back at me for, well, hanging my laundry on the balcony."

"She is a piece of work."

"I think she's just bored. Her husband seems to be out of the house all day doing god knows what. I've never even seen them talk to each other. If she's sleeping with the neighbors, I almost wouldn't blame her."

"Sloane! You're bad." Charlie's face lit up at the possible gossip, and she tilted forward in her chair to lean over the balcony. "You know a lot about these people, having barely met them."

"When all you have is a window and—" she almost said *a ghost* "—barely anyone to talk to, you begin to study everything you can see. I am a caged animal, but in a way, the neighbors are the ones being watched at the zoo. We're always home, we see all."

"Who is *we*?" Charlie asked, but when Sloane tightened her lips, she changed the topic. "Too bad you didn't see the murder."

"I should have," Sloane said, then her voice softened. She looked behind her into the townhouse, but Alanis's ghost wasn't there. "I should have."

She thought back to the night Alanis was out of the house. She'd heard a scream when doing laundry in the middle of the night, but she'd thought maybe it was the Pacillis, so besides her initial panic, she'd paid it little mind. But was it? If she could hear the scream, and it was Alanis, then it must have been close by. Did anyone else hear it, or was it just herself? Why was there blood in her back yard?

Her brain began to muddle again, and she tuned in to Charlie chattering on about some dude at her bar. "They're all disgusting, you know. I hate living in the middle of nowhere."

Sloane sighed and promised herself she'd pay attention to her friend. Charlie was the only friend she'd kept in the divorce. Everyone else was Brian's because they all hung out in groups and Sloane stayed home.

Her eyes went up and down the street and she saw Rick leaving his house with his dog again. Sloane said out loud, "I wonder if he has a wife or girlfriend."

Charlie looked toward the large man and said, "He's not your type. I'm pretty sure he's gay, given the adorable bow on the Dachshund and how happy he is."

"Oh gosh. I wonder why that didn't occur to me."

"You can't know these things unless you ask. I just have a good gaydar from working in service for years."

Sloane considered this for a sec. If Rick was indeed gay and had a partner or husband, were either of them living in the house the day Alanis's body was discovered in a car right outside their door? Sloane asked this last part out loud.

"It was Jackson's car, though." Charlie reminded her.

"What?"

"It was Jackson's car. Not that guy's. What'd you call him? Rick's."

Rick heard his name and looked up toward Sloane's balcony. She waved at him, but he turned the other way, toward the forest.

Just then, the door of the house next to Rick's opened, and a man wearing a toolbelt stepped out. He waved at Rick then closed and locked the door behind himself. He turned left and walked past Rick's and Jackson's houses, then picked up the pace until he'd entered the unfinished townhouse at the entrance to the neighborhood.

Peculiar, Sloane thought. *Why is a construction worker way over there?*

Nina came out onto her front porch. Sloane whispered "shush," and Charlie stopped chattering about random things. They watched Nina stare at Rick's back as he and his dog entered the forest. She'd just missed the construction worker.

Nina put her hands on her hips and tracked Rick's movement until he was out of sight. Then, she looked up and down the street, catching sight of the construction worker just as he entered the building he belonged to.

Sloane and Charlie tucked their heads down. Although they were still in view, they hoped they'd barely be noticeable from Nina's vantage point.

Nina's eyes retreated and seemed to linger for a minute on Jackson's door, and then she turned around and walked back inside her house.

"I wonder what her problem is?" whispered Charlie.

"Probably heard you say Rick the way Rick heard it, and she needed to be nosy and stalk everyone."

"You need to go to that meeting and cut them all down a privacy notch. Fight for laundry rights or whatever, but also push for extra soundproofing in the exterior walls. If anything, it will stop the arguing from echoing into your house."

"I like the Pacillis," Sloane laughed. "They're just nervous about the new baby."

Charlie nodded, then changed the subject. "So, Jackson is available for dating now?"

Sloane laughed at her boldness. "Jackson was always single. Alanis was a second cousin."

"Really? She was hot. I'm surprised he didn't want to hit that."

"That would be questionable, but who knows – maybe he did."

They stared at Jackson's front porch for a time, Sloane almost willing him to come out and wave hello. She wanted to see his face again.

Charlie snapped her out of it with, "Do you think he did it?"

"Jackson? No," Sloane said quickly, but she still was not sure. She repeated more confidently, "No."

"So, who did? You live miles away from town. Any stranger in your neighborhood would have been noticed by someone, yes? Alanis went out for a walk but ended up in the trunk of Jackson's car? It makes no sense."

"Well, if he was the killer, putting her in his own trunk would be a silly place to hide the body, right?" Sloane didn't think Jackson was that stupid. She hoped he wasn't, anyway, or she was a really bad judge of character.

"So, maybe someone set him up?"

"Maybe. Possibly." Sloane didn't know enough about his life to figure out what kind of skeletons he had in his closet. She decided to ask him more questions at dinner. She said as much to Charlie.

"He's coming over for dinner?" Charlie shrieked. "I don't know if that's safe!"

Nina's door opened again. Sloane shushed Charlie and sat quietly. This time, Nina did spot them and waved, then retreated back into her home. Charlie lowered her voice and whispered, "You have got to tell me about this date."

"It's not a date! But I'll tell you about it if you quit drawing attention to us already."

"Deal!"

CHAPTER SEVENTEEN

For an agoraphobic, Sloane had endured a ton of social interaction. She mused this to herself as she retrieved a bottle of wine from her pantry. Was wine too forward for a not-a-date date? She wondered.

Her dryer was still on the fritz, and after Charlie left, she'd called a repairman, but it would be weeks until someone could get out there. Her skivvies were currently hung just inside the window of the laundry room, chilly air blowing past them and continuing down into the kitchen. Before Jackson came over, she would go back upstairs and close the window.

At seven, the sounds of light tapping at the front door made her heart skip a beat, but she forced her shoulders to relax. She calculated the odds that it was Jackson, not due until seven thirty, or Nina, who might show up any time. She decided Jackson must be early, and she carefully and slowly undid the three bolts on the door, creaking the door open just a bit to peek out. When she saw his smile, she eased up and swung the door open. He held out wine and a potted plant.

"Took you awhile," Jackson said, "You have to think about cutting back on the bolts and instead building a laser beam alarm system with a camera or something."

"It would help if I had a peep hole," Sloane laughed, "What's with the plant?"

Jackson blushed. "I didn't want to be presumptuous, but I noticed you don't have a lot of the outside world inside your house, so I thought I'd bring you something living to take care of. It's like a housewarming present." He handed it to her. "And it's less commitment than a kitten."

Sloane thanked him and eyed the plant, looking for the little label that would tell her what it was and how to take care of it. "Aloe," she mused, "this will be great for when I burn myself on the stove." She snapped off the end of a leaf and smelled the fragrance of nature's healing plant, letting the liquid ooze down her fingers.

"Is that what it is?" Jackson seemed sheepish. "It caught my attention at the grocery store and reminded me of you."

"Why? Because it's sharp and prickly and is filled with creamy goo inside?"

Jackson laughed. "No, because it was sitting alone on a shelf and had a clearance sticker on it."

Sloane swatted him and closed the door, first peering out at the road to watch for neighbors.

Jackson caught this movement. "No one followed me here, if that's what you're worried about. Your secrets are safe with me."

"You're funny. Come upstairs. The Chinese just arrived, which is great because I didn't think you'd be here until seven thirty."

"I was bored," Jackson said.

Sloane sensed something else behind his statement. Perhaps loneliness, or fear. Hopefully not an innate desire for more blood.

Over dinner they talked about work, which Sloane figured was a customary thing to do on a first date-but-not-a-date. Jackson talked about software development, and the bureaucracy of working for the state government. He hedged a bet that most of the residents of their little neighborhood worked at either the bank or the government, Jefferson City's two major—and boring--industries. He envied Sloane's remote job for the Feds.

"It's not that great, really. It's just boring admin work. Someone calls saying their laptop was stolen, and I relay the message to the real people in IT or whatever. That sort of thing. Boring," Sloane reiterated.

"Couldn't they just contact the IT department directly?"

"It's the feds, they always need a go-between."

"You should just set up a software tool that automatically redirets all messages, then you can sit their and collect your federal pension."

That wouldn't be a very ethical thing to do, Jackson."

"I'm not much of an ethical guy," Jackson winked at her.

What did that mean, she wondered.

A soft knock sounded at the front door. The hairs on Sloane's neck shot up and she gripped the table. Jackson caught this movement before she could take a relaxing inhale. "Would you like me to get it," he offered.

"I, uh," Sloane gathered her wits. "Sure, thanks." She followed behind him but remained on the stairs.

He unbolted the three locks like it wasn't unusual at all, then swung the door wide open, with no hedging nor peeking through the crack. She envied him.

Officer Drew Byrd stood at the front door with his right arm poised to knock again. He put it down when he saw Jackson. He tilted his head in the house and spotted Sloane on the stairs. "Everything alright here?"

She realized her face was probably still stricken with panic, so she plastered a smile on it, instead.

"It's fine," Sloane relaxed. "What can I do for you Officer Byrd?"

Jackson held the door with his right hand, and put his left on his hip, as though irritated with the visit.

"Mr. Stone, you've been asked to remain in your house or your workplace and not go anywhere else," Drew said to him, an air of lion-like competition seeping from his scowl.

"I'm directly across the road, officer." Jackson's grimace grew to match Drew's.

They eyed each other for a split second before Drew continued talking. "A neighbor called me with a concern. I'm just following up on it."

"Nina." Sloane crossed her arms and shook her head.

Drew looked from Jackson to Sloane. "I can't divulge the identity of people who call the police," he said.

Sloane waved a hand at him. "You don't need to. Will that be all, Officer Byrd?" She decided that if Drew was going to be formal, she could be formal, too.

He flinched, but ever so slightly, then turned back to Jackson "Mr. Stone, it would be in your best interest to remain at home like you've been asked, if you'd like to prevent this from happening in the future."

"Yeah, I got it. Sloane and I were just cleaning up from dinner anyway."

"I've got the rest of the dishes, Jackson." Sloane smiled at him.

"If you're sure."

Both men wore their emotions on their sleeve. They were obviously frustrated with each other. Sloane thought at any minute they might break into some animalistic cage fight.

Or a dance off, she laughed at herself.

Drew stepped back out of the doorway, allowing Jackson to pass by him.

Jackson smiled up at Sloane and, with a charisma that felt excessive, said, "Thanks for a lovely evening."

Drew kept his eyes on Sloane as Jackson passed him and went down the steps toward his house. As soon as he was out of earshot, Drew spoke. "It's in your best interest to be careful with whom you spend your time. There is a murder investigation going on right now."

Sloane's irritation grew, but she hid it well. "Will that be all, Officer? Thanks for your concern." She approached the door to shut and lock it.

Drew muttered, "Sorry." It seemed to lack sincerity, however.

Sloane closed the door and triple-bolted it.

CHAPTER EIGHTEEN

When Sloane slumped back onto her main floor, Alanis was hovering near the balcony windows again, peering out through the sheers.

"At some point, you have to try and remember what happened," Sloane stated, boldly. She wondered when it had happened that she'd gone from fear to comfort at having a ghost in her home. It may have occured sometime around the point where the living beings in her life became more annoying than friendly. At least Alanis' ghost didn't seem envious of the random men in her life, nor nosy about her private goings-on.

She wondered what she was hiding from anymore. Perhaps it was now the living who scared her more.

"I don't remember," Alanis's voice echoed as she floated. Again, her mouth didn't seem to move. Sloane wondered if she were imagining the voices.

Sloane approached the opposite side of the dining table from Alanis but kept an eye on the apparition through the side of her eye. She began clearing plates.

"Jackson," Alanis's voice hummed.

The hairs on Sloane's arms tingled. "Did he do this to you?" She tried to ask as casually as possible.

She did not want to be falling for a murderer.

Alanis's ghost began to fade away.

"Wait," Sloane said, and she looked at Alanis's face. The ghost's head turned, and her cold dead eyes stared directly into Sloane's soul.

Sloane shivered and repeated, "Wait, please. I have to know. Did he do this to you?"

"Charlie," the ghost echoed with lips closed.

"Charlie what? Charlie what?!" Sloane cried out, but Alanis was gone.

A familiar knock sounded at the door. *Shave and a haircut, ten pence.*

Charlie. Alanis was just informing her that Charlie was here.

Sloane walked down the stairs muttering, "Well, it's nice to have a surveillance system, I guess."

She swung the door wide open to her best friend.

Charlie stepped back, mouth agape. "You didn't panic! You didn't peek through the crack in the door! Babe," she stepped in for a big hug. She took the door from Sloane, shut it, and bolted it herself. She didn't even let Sloane explain. "Is Jackson here with you? He's good for you if he helps you be less nervous," she looked up the stairs as if hoping to see the cute neighbor.

"No," Sloane breathed. She was a bit stunned at herself for whipping the door open like that. She wasn't about to tell Charlie that it was a creepy ghost who had calmed her nerves.

Charlie marched upstairs and grabbed a bottle of wine from under the cupboard. She nodded toward the balcony. "Let's go sit," she said, "and see if anything interesting happens in the 'hood tonight. I'm completely addicted to the TV show of your life now."

Sloane felt at ease and moved out onto the balcony with little trepidation. She wondered if it was because of her best friend's presence, or that of her new roommate, the ghostly Alanis. Sloane wondered if Alanis would remain after the murder was solved, or if not, might Sloane benefit from having a real, live roommate to keep her calm and help her outside?

The sun dropped below the horizon and the sky quickly grew dark. Sloane offered to turn on the balcony light before she stepped out, but Charlie held her hand up to silence her.

Rick's door was opening up the street. Nina emerged, looking nervously up and down the road, and she sprinted across to her house. She hadn't seen Sloane and Charlie in the dark.

"Naughty," mused Charlie, "Now she's hitting on the other single dude? I wonder what they were up to?"

"Nah. Probably planning for tomorrow night's super important HOA meeting," Sloane muttered. "All the good shit is going to go down there, from what I hear."

"You need to attend it, Sloane. It might be fun. Or funny, either way."

"Uh, no. I don't do people-ing, and I definitely don't do hanging out at a home of someone I barely tolerate."

Charlie smiled at this and watched the road, then wondered aloud, "Besides the laundry issue, why do you despise her so?"

Sloane had to think about it. For all she knew Nina was just a lonely housewife, there was nothing particularly egregious to dislike about that. "I don't know," she finally said. "The woman just rubs me the wrong way."

"Ah, like a date that's bad at sex. I've been there."

Laughing ensued. Jackson must have heard it from inside his house, because he opened his door a short time later and took careful steps out onto his front porch. He spotted the outline of Sloane and Charlie's shadow, and he waved up at them. "Not laughing about me, I hope?"

"What if we are," asked Charlie. "Are you going to come here and do something about it?"

Sloane punched her, then to Jackson said, "Excuse my friend. She never learned manners."

Jackson laughed, then frowned. "I wish I could join you, but I don't need Officer Blah in my business."

"*That's* what I dislike about Nina," Sloane said under her breath. "She's probably the one who called Drew."

"That'd do it, cock-blocking your date like that." Charlie said it loud enough for Jackson to hear, and both Jackson and Sloane blushed.

Ken Smythe walked out from around the corner. Jackson spotted him, pointed, and called up to the women, "That's my cue to retreat. Can't be seen outside."

Jackson waved and went back inside, as Ken slowly passed between their two houses. A light went out in Rick's living room window. Nina came out onto her porch, just missing Jackson's door clicking into place. Her husband seemed surprised or irritated to see her. Nina took a sideways glance up and down the street. She spotted the women in the dark and then forced Ken to give her a smooch. It seemed awkward and unnatural. They walked into their house together.

"Oh, to be young and in love and sleeping with all of your male neighbors," said Charlie softly.

Sloane lightly punched her in the arm again. "You're so bad."

Charlie looked over Sloane's shoulder and asked, "Who is that?"

In the other direction, the construction workers had long gone for the day, but the white Plymouth remained. A worker came out of the unfinished townhouses, and Sloane recognized him. "That's Jose. He seems to always stay late." She wondered if maybe Jose was the supervisor and stayed late and arrived early.

Jose went to the white car, put his hat and vest in the trunk, and removed a small bag from the depths. Then he peered up and down the street, not seeing the two women sitting in the darkened balcony. He tucked the small bag under his arm and took a fast walk back to the unfinished duplex, the lightless shell of its wood and weather-barrier blocking the rest of their view.

"Strange," said Sloane. "I wonder if he's trying to get the work done quicker and stays extra hours."

"That doesn't make much sense," said Charlie. "Construction hours are fairly regimented. They've already had a full day here, haven't they?"

"His was the first car here this morning."

"Do you think-" Charlie paused to verbalize a thought and whispered, "-do you think he's living there?"

Sloane thought about it. He was always around, and there had been odd movements in the building which had startled Sloane quite often. "I wouldn't want to presume, but it would make sense. He's always here," she said.

"I wonder how long that's been going on."

"If he's squatting in the unfinished building, he would have been here on the weekend, when Alanis died."

"He might have heard the same scream you did. I wonder if the police talked to him."

Sloane thought back. Jose had purposefully ducked out before the cops had come to speak with her. Then she'd seen him bolt again when the inspectors did their official rounds later. Was it just that he was working illegally, or was he working and squatting? Or worse, did he have something to do with Alanis's death? He'd seemed so nice and helpful, but was he?

Charlie didn't wait for an answer. "Should we go call him out?" She pulled a bottle of wine out from beside her seat and refilled her glass.

"I can't do that," Sloane stated, unequivocally accepting that her mental illness prevented her from doing something so bold. "Plus, if he's squatting there illegally, he probably doesn't want us to know that we know."

Charlie shrugged. "If he needs a place to live, you should offer him your spare room."

"You, Jackson, and these cops are more than enough people for me. Now you're inviting late-night construction workers into my house."

Sloane chose to leave out that she already kind of had a roommate, Alanis's ghost.

Charlie laughed. "He can't be creepy! He's been in your house to hang things."

"How do I know he's not Alanis's killer?"

Charlie thought for a moment. "Construction killers don't stuff bodies into trunks. They can just hammer you on the head while you sleep and leave you be."

"This is not making me want a construction roommate any time soon, Charlie."

CHAPTER NINETEEN

Frustrated voices carried up between the alley way, slightly muffled by a hard rain pummeling the windows. Sloane assumed it was the Pacillis again, fighting over baby names, or maybe which baby gate to buy. She languished in bed until the noise died down, not wanting to go downstairs and overhear precise and specific words. As fun as neighborhood gossip was, she felt it wasn't her business to listen in on their harmless tiff.

A rat-a-tat knock at the door sounded. Not the customary bang bang bang three times that usually happened with strangers, nor was it the '*shave and a haircut*' her friends used. This was different, more like a drumroll with a pretend cymbal addition added on at the end. It was so unexpected and unusual, that Sloane surprised herself by not panicking.

She pulled a white bathrobe over her t-shirt and booty shorts and padded down the two levels to open the door.

"Jackson," she said to her neighbor. He stood on her porch, dressed in a loose suit. She suspected he was on his way to work. The top of his chest peaked out of his open top buttons, and she caught her throat as she admired his sharp collar bone.

"Hey, Sloane." He shuffled his feet, appearing nervous. "I don't really know what I'm doing here. I just wanted to check to make sure you were okay."

"I'm good. Why wouldn't I be? By the way, I like your knock." She smiled at the door as she said this.

"You like that, huh? I thought you would. I've noticed you..." he thought of his words carefully, "--don't like answering the door."

"Oh, that. I-"

He cut her off. "Hey, no need for your life story now. I just wanted to make sure you were here. That's all."

"Again, why wouldn't I be?" Sloane felt comfortable enough in his presence to force her head out the door. She peered up and down the street, but nothing seemed amiss.

"I heard arguing. I didn't know if you had a guy over or something." Jackson took the same opportunity to look over her shoulder and into the house.

"No, not me." She gestured to her neighbors' house. "You're probably hearing the Pacillis. They adore each other but they bicker all the time."

"No, this wasn't them. I would recognize their fights. I distinctly heard other voices, and a different language."

"Oh?" Sloane thought back. Had the rain on her windows muffled the voices enough that she only assumed it was her next-door neighbors? Perhaps the wind had carried the sounds from further away. "Well," she smiled and shrugged, "it wasn't coming from my house. Thanks for checking."

"Hey, just making sure."

"Would you like to come in for a coffee?" Sloane realized they'd been standing at the door all this time, Jackson on her cold front stoop. Although he was under the cement balcony, the dampness would still be seeping into his bones from the chilly rain.

"I would," he smiled. "But I can't. I have to get to work. Also, I don't want Officer Birdbrain to spot me cavorting around the neighborhood and away from my stations."

"Hey, give Drew a break," said Sloane.

"You're on a first name basis with the guy? I see how it is." Jackson frowned, but a sly smile edged at the corner of his mouth.

Sloane rolled her eyes. "He's just trying to do his job. Go easy on him."

Jackson shrugged, the grin still on his face. "Let's catch up at the end of the day, okay? Would you like to come over to my place? That way I stay legit with your police officer friend."

"I-- " Sloane looked across the street at Jackson's front door.

Across the wide suburban street.

With cars.

And people.

And air. And sky, and birds and trees and plains and living and dead and a vast expanse of unknowable universe that she couldn't comprehend. She stepped back into her house.

"Woah, you're white as a ghost. Hey, it's no big deal at all." Jackson put his hands up and stepped back toward the steps.

At the word 'ghost,' Sloane instinctively looked behind her to see if Alanis was around. "It's just that-"

"It's okay, Sloane. No worries," Jackson stated. He seemed to force a smile on his face, and he stepped down from her porch and into the blowing rain. "I'll catch you at the next mail mixup," he said, holding a hand up as though in a gesture of peace.

Sloane smiled, waved shyly, and closed the door. She leaned against the back of it, hating herself and her flawed brain.

CHAPTER TWENTY

The rest of the morning was ghostless. Sloane logged into multiple layers of government security and answered simple requests from random agents out in the field. By lunch, she needed a mental break. So she gathered the will to hang some freshly washed sheets on her balcony. Draped in a heavy sweater and leggings, she let the cool breeze hit her face, intending to calm herself, before emptying her basket of wet bedclothes.

"Dryer still not working?" Nina startled her from the street. Sloane hadn't noticed her looming presence, but Nina's icy platitudes and fake, plastic smile suddenly made the weather feel like a burden again.

Sloane continued hanging pillowcases on part of the balcony that she shared with the empty duplex next door. The For Sale sign had flipped over in the wind. Sloane didn't bother to reach over flip it back. If there was any way to delay new neighbors, she'd take it. "Yup, seems that way," Sloane forced out. She moved on to some fitted sheets.

"I could send Ken over to look at it," Nina offered, hopefully.

Sloane shuddered. She hardly knew Ken. She took a breath and said, "That's okay, I'm ordering a new one. The repairman thinks rats may have eaten through the belts while it was in storage."

Nina's fake disposition now turned real, and ugly. While she attempted to maintain the smile plastered across her face, her vitriol began to slip out. "Hanging laundry outside goes against the HOA policies."

Sloane didn't need to hear this again. She'd heard it a million times. She'd received all Nina's notes taped to her door. Telling Sloane about the arbitrary rule yet again wasn't going to instantly have a new dryer arrive, nor would it give her the ability to dry her clothes without doing it the old-fashioned way. Sloane gripped the fitted sheet a little tighter. She was getting tired of the outside again and starting to feel dizzy.

She spoke through gritted teeth. "Don't worry about that. I'm bringing a petition around to change that particular ordinance."

That was a lie. How could she petition anyone when she couldn't leave her house? She didn't know how she was going to back that threat up. Maybe Charlie would take a petition around for her.

Nina scowled. "Then I look forward to seeing you at the meeting tonight."

"Sure," said Sloane, unconvincingly. "See you tonight."

Just then, an old red Pontiac Firebird turned into the neighborhood from the underused back entrance and parked in front of Rick's duplex. Nina's attention was piqued, and Sloane took the opportunity to step back into her house.

From the open doorway, she watched Officer Byrd exit the vehicle and walk up to the door of the house next to Rick's, the one that seemed occupied but which Sloane had never seen a neighbor.

Nina squealed. "Oh good, Drew is here! Maybe I can get him to talk some sense into you."

"What's he doing over there, I wonder." Sloane mused this through the open door.

"That's his house," Nina said, as she started walking up the street.

Sloane stared. *His house? Since when?*

Sloane watched Nina approach Drew's door and knock, but he didn't answer. She tried again half a minute later, but nothing.

Oh well, if Nina were knocking on my door I probably wouldn't answer, either. But then again, if he has a house like mine with no peep hole, does he know it's Nina, or does he not answer anyone?

Sloane took one last look around the neighborhood. There were no signs of life save for Nina, now appearing upset and retreating back to her own house. Right before Nina disappeared into her front door, she paused to glance over at the unfinished townhouses next to Sloane, then she went inside.

Sloane shut and locked the balcony door, hoping the rain had stopped for the rest of the day. She'd ignored work for too long, so it was time to log in again and earn her keep.

Sloane was lucky her government job was entirely remote. It was rare for someone in central intelligence to never have to visit an office. But she wasn't any kind of spy, thank goodness. She was just a boring admin, fact-checking random papers and fixing issues when the real heroes had requests. While she had high security clearance, Sloane never felt particularly important, her job was dull. She was merely glad to have a steady paycheck and government healthcare.

Healthcare I should probably try to use to fix my agoraphobia at some point, she teased herself as she climbed up to her third-floor office.

After a few hours of mindless problem-solving, another knock sounded at the door. The hairs on her neck stood up a little and she groaned. Logging out of her virtual private network was a pain in the butt, but it had to be done when someone else was in the house. It's one tiny part of the reason her and Brian had to break up. He couldn't stand being kicked out of the house completely when she had to work off-hours, but she couldn't bring herself to leave home to go into an office.

On her way down from the third floor, Sloane peered out the balcony window to make sure there were no new cars in the neighborhood. A UPS or FedEx truck would have been fine, too, but she wasn't expecting any deliveries. While Sloane prided herself on getting to a point where she could tolerate some of her more annoying neighbors—*mainly Nina*, she laughed to herself--she didn't want any new people to enter her life just yet.

She unbolted the door, listening through it to see if she could hear anything that would give the visitor away. She pried open the door slightly to look out. It was Drew.

"I'm sorry to bother you, Sloane."

"It's no trouble," she lied. "Something I can help you with?"

Drew looked over his right shoulder toward Nina and the Pacilli's duplex. "May I come in?"

"Sure," Sloane smiled and widened the door. She stepped back so Drew could enter. He took the door from her and closed it himself. She was both grateful for the outside world disappearing, but also a bit nervous because part of it had come inside.

Drew stepped from foot to foot and ran a nervous hand through his hair. "Ms. Smythe asked me to-"

"Nina." Sloane rolled her eyes. "Is this about the laundry?"

Drew shrugged and coughed. "The HOA has rules."

Sloane felt herself grow irate. "Are they police rules? Are you taking me to jail? This is absurd."

"I'm sorry. You're right, this isn't my issue. In all honesty I told her I'd talk to you just because I wanted to check up on you and make sure you were okay."

Sloane's tension abated, but only slightly. *Why is everyone so concerned about my safety this morning?* "I'm actually thinking of starting a petition to allow air-dried laundry."

"So, you'll go to Nina's meeting, then?"

She shook her head. *No, no.* "Probably not," was all she said.

Drew stepped back toward the door, then suddenly seemed to get a bright idea. "Why don't you let me look at your dryer?"

"It's no use, rats ate through the wires underneath. I'm going to order a new one, I just need to balance the budget. New home mortgage and all, you know how it is."

"Okay," Drew said helplessly. "Just be careful. Nina is probably already asking the property management company to fine you. Fines could end up costing more than a new dryer."

"I'll take the bill to my lawyer," Sloane lied. She didn't have a lawyer. She and her ex hadn't even used a divorce lawyer in their amicable split.

Drew opened the door and Sloane took it from him, leaning on the edge of it. He paused at the doorstep and turned. "You cn have mine."

"I can have your what?"

"My dryer. I have two now because -" he paused again, and his face grew concerned.

Sloane finished his sentence for him, "-You just bought the house up the street." She looked in the direction of the duplex he'd now share with Rick.

"You know about that, huh?" He attempted a smile.

"Nina told me." The two of them looked over to see Nina outside on her porch, faking watering her plants again. Sloane sighed.

"She's going to drown those things if-"

"It's a long story-"

"I don't need an explanation for why you bought a house," Sloane interjected, smiling. "This neighborhood is great. Welcome."

Drew seemed relieved. "Anyway, I'm staying at my old place until the construction crews fix up a few things, and I already have a washer dryer there that I can move later. You can take the new one from the townhouse."

"I'll buy it off you in installments," insisted Sloane.

"You can take it for free, really. I'll bring it over on a dolly next time I'm in the neighborhood."

Sloane thanked him and he left.

She shut the door and turned, almost right into Alanis's ghost.

"Fuck," she gasped.

The ghost shifted out of her way, then floated languidly up the stairs.

Sloane shrugged and followed. "Well, at least we know what the toolbelt guy was doing way up the street earlier. That's one mystery solved,"

"One," the ghost echoed.

"I gotta bake some more stress cookies," Sloane stated, and headed into the kitchen. The ghost hovered, just keeping her company.

CHAPTER TWENTY-ONE

In the early evening, Charlie, having sloughed off a slow Thursday night at the pub, used her key to get into Sloane's house.

Sloane was busy retrieving cookies from the oven. Although she heard the door, she didn't tense as much as usual. She took a quick look for Alanis' ghost, but she was alone.

"Babe, it's just me," Charlie called as she bounded up the stairs. "I thought you might like someone on your side."

"On my side for what?" Sloane took her oven mitts off to give her friend a hug.

"For the HOA meeting. It's tonight, right?" Charlie said this as she pulled from the hug and stared Sloane in the face.

Sloane paled and felt her heartbeat thump in her chest. "Oh no, I'm not going there."

"I thought you might say that, so I brought some supplies." Sloane noticed a large bag in Charlie's hand, which Charlie proceeded to empty onto the counter. "First, a pair of dark sunglasses, so the world can't see your eyes and you can't see the world. The sun should be completely set by the time we walk over." Sloane's grip on Charlie's shoulder tightened. She clutched her heart with her other hand. "Also," Charlie pulled another item out of her bag, "An umbrella! To hold over your shoulder so the world behind you has no access. Remember when you used to carry an umbrella with Brian?"

Sloane felt as if her stomach would fall into the floor. She leaned back against the kitchen island. She did remember. As her agoraphobia had worsened, these little quirks became commonplace. Brian had been patient with all of them, until he wasn't anymore. She'd tried to explain to him that she couldn't tell the difference between the living and the dead, but that only made him fuss over her mental health.

Charlie pulled her out of the memory. "And I'll be beside you the entire time, if you want to keep your eyes closed, and-"

"Charlie-" Sloane blew out her name as though she were huffing cold air in the arctic. Her knees weakened, and Charlie grabbed her arm.

"Hey, babe, I've got you. I've always got you."

Sloane sunk into Charlie's body like a lost child. They moved toward the couch and Charlie set her friend down deep into the soft cushions. Sloane took five deep breaths and recovered her composure, as Charlie went to the kitchen for some water.

"You're right," Sloane admitted. "If I can't make it two doors over for a stupid HOA meeting in which to defend my God-given right to hang my underwear on my personal property, then what is the point of being a homeowner and living the dream?" Sloane's sarcasm was dripping, but there was an honest truth behind her shaky words.

"Hey, if you really can't swing it, I'll go for you! I'll tell everyone I'm your private assistant and you don't make personal appearances for such trivial people."

Sloane laughed. She took the glass of water from Charlie, gulping it like she hadn't hydrated in days.

A knock sounded at the door. Sloane was winded from the earlier panic, so she merely waved at the door semi-consciously, and Charlie went downstairs to answer it.

Subdued voices could be heard wafting up the staircase.

"Well, hello there," Charlie.

"Hey, I'm Jackson." Jackson's smooth and charming voice floated up the stairs like poetry. Sloane felt butterflies in her stomach.

"I know who you are. How may I service you?" Charlie was a constant flirt, but guys ate it up.

Sloane furrowed her lip and rolled her eyes as she yelled down to the door. "Hey guys, if you're done, I'm up here."

They both climbed up the stairs, Charlie informing Jackson she was caring for the wounded. Jackson eyed Sloane with concern. While she'd never fully told him about her condition, Sloane had a feeling he was about to find out.

#

She was right. Not a few minutes later, Charlie was regaling Jackson with stories of her incapacitated friend, and how many times she'd come to Sloane's rescue. "My poor girl," Charlie cooed. "She'd have no idea what happens out in the real world were it not for me." As she said the words 'real world' she glanced over her shoulder at the balcony door and whispered the words.

Jackson glanced at Sloane, but it was clear he could not articulate what he wanted to ask.

"Agoraphobia," said Sloane, and took a sip of her water. *And a fear of the undead sneaking into my house.*

His face calmed, and he took the word into his head and bounced it around a bit. Jackson nodded. After a moment, he said, "That would explain quite a bit."

Charlie gave a flirty grin and turned back to Sloane. "See? he gets it!"

"Just because he understands the word," remarked Sloane, "Doesn't mean he gets it."

"Hey, I'm right here," Jackson interjected, faking offense. He winked at Charlie. A flash of jealousy tinged at Sloane's consciousness, but she quenched it. He was under suspicion of murder, after all. She liked him, but she didn't *like*-like him. *That would be silly.*

Jackson said, "Okay, so I just stopped by to see if you were heading to Nina's HOA meeting." He eyed her up from toe to hair before adding, "But with this new information I can presume that you're not, so-"

"Now, hold on a minute," insisted Charlie. "I've almost got her ready to go!" She moved into the kitchen to grab her bag of supposed agoraphobic tricks.

Sloane put her hand on her forehead and laid back further into the cushions, both embarrassed about her current condition and wondering why her friend thought these tricks would help her at all.

Jackson watched her, obviously confused as to the proper move to make.

"Look," said Sloane. "Drew - I mean Officer Byrd -" she stole a glance at Jackson, who suddenly looked frustrated. "Drew is lending me his dryer. This laundry problem with Nina will all be solved by the weekend. I don't even need to attend this meeting." She laid her head back onto the sofa and rubbed her temples.

"Oh, I see," was all Jackson said.

"Ooo, a dryer! Noice," said Charlie, but then she continued. "This doesn't solve your problems, though."

"My problem is the laundry. Everything else is cool with the HOA."

Charlie put a hand on her hip and pointed a finger. "No, Sloane, this doesn't help you." She said this while looking sidewards toward the balcony, and then repeated it with more emphasis. "You know, your *problem*." She elongated the word for Sloane, who was glued to the sofa as though it were the world's strongest magnet.

Sloane sighed and crawled off the sofa. "I know, you're right. Let's do it. Let's go. Maybe I'll learn something about the HOA that I didn't know before. God knows I didn't read that 300-page manual when I moved in."

Jackson laughed. "I used mine as a doorstop while I was hauling my furniture inside."

Charlie squealed in delight and ran over to her bag of tricks, offering Sloane the dark sunglasses. "This is going to be so much fun!" Then she started down the stairs.

"Oh yeah," Sloane breathed after her. "A real hoot."

"We'll each be at your side," said Jackson reassuringly. "We've got your back."

"Which do you have, my side or my back? I feel like I need to be flanked."

"Umbrella," stated Charlie, handing her the device. She began the trip downstairs.

Sloane took deep breaths, and Jackson began searching her cabinets in the kitchen. Sloane asked, "What are you looking for?"

"A Tupperware container, for these cookies."

"Oh, you want to bring them?"

"I thought that's what they were for."

"Silly man. I bake because it calms my nerves. I don't actually do very much with the results." Sloane reached into a cabinet under the toaster and pulled out a plastic bowl. "This is all I have. My ex-husband got the Tupperware."

Jackson's jaw dropped. "What do you do with them? You don't toss them, do you? That would be a crime! You have *got* to let me know when you're baking. I'll take all your cookies!"

"Goodness. I don't know what that means," Sloane faked fanning herself and winked at him. He blushed.

Sloane went to descend the stairs as Jackson filled the bowl with cookies. As she took the first steps, the beats of her heart started ringing in her ears. She slowed her pace, but the thumping grew louder in her ears. Charlie spotted her slowing down and ascended up to hold her hand. Jackson came down from behind her and put a hand on the side of her shoulder. "Cool?"

The beating diminished. It was still audible, but with the flank of soldiers surrounding her, she could think again. "Cool," she breathed.

They stayed together in a group and continued down the stairs. When it was time to open the door, Charlie took the reins and kept looking back at Sloane, who had placed the sunglasses on her face. She opened the door and the crisp outside air whooshed in, even catching Charlie off guard. "It's a chilly one tonight," she smiled. "You okay?"

Jackson moved his arm from Sloane's shoulder down to her back. His hand felt warm and comforting.

"Ready," she sighed, and Charlie moved back to hold the door open.

Sloane walked out onto stoop and looked down at her front porch. It was just like the balcony above, only it needed to be swept. She also noted the lack of curb appeal. For a moment, she imagined that maybe one day she could invest in some potted plants to decorate with. Then she could overwater them and be a busybody like Nina, too. She laughed at herself.

Charlie and Jackson, although they didn't know what she was laughing at, chuckled as well. Soon Sloane was giggling at her predicament more than anything else. Jackson's grasp of her backside eased, but he didn't let go. Charlie took the umbrella and opened it.

"Look at me, I'm a wreck," laughed Sloane.

"No," insisted Charlie. "It's more like this - you're just too important to go anywhere alone."

"That's right," insisted Jackson. "We're your bodyguards. Come on, one more big move to make." He moved ahead of Sloane down the first front step. He didn't let go of her, but instead slid his hand from behind her back to her left hip. He signaled with the bowl of cookies that she should keep moving, as though she were an airplane, and he was the signalman.

Charlie slid her arm around Sloane's back to replace Jackson's.

She felt safe in both their arms as they descended the steps to the sidewalk, but she also felt quite ridiculous. "I'm going to need a three-way every time I have to go anywhere."

Jackson crooked his head to the side. "I don't think anyone would complain about that."

Charlie chimed in, pushing Sloane from behind. "Sounds awesome but make it two dudes! That's the legit kind of threesome!"

Jackson frowned.

Sloane was so busy giggling at both of them joking with each other, she soon found herself on the sidewalk with little more than a rapidity to her heartbeat and a deepened breath. The hairs on her flesh were still smooth, save for the chilly air touching her body. She stopped to think about her position and turned to stare up behind her. Like a child, she stated, "That's my house."

Jackson and Charlie looked up at it too, as though it were a national monument. "Hm-mm," Charlie agreed, and pushed Sloane further down the sidewalk.

As they got farther from the house, although it was mere steps, it began to feel like miles. The road was still clear of spirits living or dead, but the outside was getting to her now. Sloane's breathing shallowed and her steps became shorter. She mouthed a soft, "Tell more jokes."

Jackson scrambled, "uh... a termite walks into a bar and says 'hey, is the bar*tender* here?'"

"That's not what she means, dummy," Charlie cursed, still pushing Sloane from behind.

"Well, I'm not going to hurl random insults at you for the sake of entertainment," retorted Jackson.

"This is good. This is great," Sloane mumbled, forcing a smile.

"Come on, we're already here."

They had passed the Pacilli's front step and arrived at the Smythe's right next door. It had felt like an hour but was mere seconds. Sloane abandoned their hands and raced up the stairs to the door, confusing Charlie and Jackson for a brief moment. She knew the layout of Nina Smythe's townhouse would be identical to her own. She found comfort in facing the same door she used every day, keeping the outside behind her. She knocked loudly, in the hopes that this would bring the host to the door faster and she could just get inside. Although hanging out with relative strangers was the last thing Sloane wanted to do, the absolute worst part was over. Now she'd just have to endure a meeting, but at least she'd feel comfort knowing where key components of the house were. Having a bathroom or a sink handy if she began to panic again would be very useful.

It felt like Nina took forever to answer the door, and by the time she did Sloane had paled to almost translucent. Luckily, the shock involved from being stranded outside was enough to keep her quiet, so her panic attack wasn't raging and desperate.

Nina whipped open the door, spotted Sloane and seethed, "Well, hello there." She then spotted Jackson and grew even more disdainful. "And what is *he* doing here?" She completely ignored Charlie.

Sloane did not rush inside, as she wanted to do, because she didn't want to appear rude. Instead, she took a deep gasp of air and said, "This is my friend, Charlie."

Charlie chirped, "Nice to meet you." She held out her hand.

A brief sneer crossed Nina's face, then she wiped it away almost immediately. She offered a limp, clammy hand but pretended to be nice as she said, "This is an HOA meeting for the HOA members."

"I'm moving in with Sloane," Charlie lied.

Sloane smiled, wishful thinking.

"Sloane is the homeowner."

"Maybe we're lovers," Charlie replied.

Jackson, tired of standing in the cold, offered Nina the cookies and stepped inside, pulling Sloane with his strong arm on her back.

"Jackson, how thoughtful," Nina eyed them suspiciously.

Does she think there is poison in them? Sloane wondered.

"Sloane made them," he stated. It was clear he was not acknowledging Nina's distrust of him.

Nina said nothing, but stepped back and signaled with her head that they could head upstairs. "The meeting is in my living room. I trust you all know where that is." She followed them upstairs.

Already somewhat squished on Nina's purple living room sofa were Rick, Ken, and Principal Mackleby, who introduced herself as Terra. Sloane introduced Charlie, and Jackson went to the two men, shaking their hands. Charlie spotted collapsible chairs leaning against a wall, and she and Sloane set up three of them for themselves and Jackson. Nina put the bowl of cookies on the coffee table. The group on the couch just stared at it, none of them daring to move from their squished position. Terra looked especially uncomfortable.

Sloane took in the same but different surroundings. Where her kitchen island was black granite, the Smythe's was a cool metal surface, possibly stainless steel. Their walls remained the same boring apartment yellow that was custom with the home, but they had decorated it with stock art, the kind you'd find in bulk at a franchise home deco store or Walmart. None of the art appeared to have a theme with its neighbor, nor even a sense of period. One was a copy of a Mondrian nouveau-art piece, and the next was a brushed farmland. Sloane admired the eclectic tastes but didn't understand them. There was no dining table in their dining room, nor many extra appliances in their kitchen. She wondered if they ordered in every night.

Rick, Ken, and Terra tried awkwardly not to touch each other while still trying to stay comfortable. Ken's hands were in his lap. Rick's arms were clutching an armrest and the back of the sofa. Terra's arms clasped together in a serious, middle-school principal pose. With the other three across the coffee table, the seating arrangement left an oversized red recliner empty at the head of the room. Nina perched herself at the very edge of it and grasped papers from the coffee table on her knees. *Such a waste of all that cushion*, thought Sloane, *but you can really tell who the boss in this house is.*

Nina chimed, "I'm calling this meeting to order! First meeting of the Willows Creek Townhome Homeowner's Association! Who is going to take minutes?" She peered around the room, giddy with power. Everyone looked down at the floor, or at each other.

Charlie chimed in, "I'll take minutes for you."

Sloane gave an unnoticeable tap on Charlie's leg. Translation, *what the hell did you say that for?*

Nina grimaced but tried to turn it into a smile. "Perfect! Since you're not a resident and you don't get a vote -" she nearly growled, "you can focus on the minutes and nothing else."

Charlie ignored the condemnation and chirped, "I've always wanted to be a court reporter!"

She grabbed a blank notebook and pen off the table and began writing in it. She checked her watch and mouthed, "Meeting called to order at seven fourteen."

Nina smiled, happily accepting Charlie's role as her new minion. Rick leaned forward and grabbed a cookie. He seemed completely disinterested in the conversation.

Ken eyed Jackson with suspicion.

"First on the agenda, I'd like to discuss article 7, chapter 7 of the Condo Association agreement, which specifically states that the exterior presentation of the units is to remain uniform, clean and presentable to any view from the common elements of the community." It was obvious that Nina had memorized this part of the manual so she could shame Sloane.

Sloane nodded her head and reached for a cookie, which she chewed slowly while pretending to give a shit.

Nina continued. "So, I'd like to ask that we not *redecorate* our balcony railings with items going forward."

Sloane took her time chewing and staring at the cookie. "Hmm-mm. Hmm-mm." She nodded in agreement, swallowed, and let the cookie flow down her throat ever so slowly. "Laundry is not a permanent decoration, although my lace underwear would make a cute neighborhood flag." She heard Jackson's muted chuckle beside her. "Also, what about your plants? And what about the Pacilli's and their rugs they're always hanging on the - hey waitaminute-"

Sloane looked around the room. "Where are Francesca and Leonardo? They should be at this meeting."

Nina shifted in her seat. "Oh, I think they couldn't make it."

"That's weird," said Sloane. "I'm sure they're home right now. We could go knock on their door-"

"It's no big deal," said Nina. "They don't speak much English anyway."

"They speak enough, I hear them all the time." Sloane didn't like admitting to her eavesdropping, but she felt she needed to defend those who couldn't be present.

"Let's just get back to the laundry!"

Sloane's jaw dropped. "You didn't invite them!"

Nina shifted again and her face became stern. "I don't care what those people do with their balcony, I just don't want to see your Princess Leia costume all over the neighborhood."

Those people. Those *people?* Sloane was caught speechless for a moment.

She frowned and returned to the subject. "I should have a dryer by tomorrow, from Drew -" she smiled as she said this, just to note the furrowed mouth on Nina upon knowing that her obvious crush was giving Sloane a present.

Jackson coughed.

"Well good, then laundry shouldn't be an issue," Nina said fleetingly. "Now, on to internet access. Since a lot of us work remotely, I think it would be a good idea to share our connections when one of us goes out."

"Hell no," said Sloane.

Jackson shook his head as well.

Rick and Principal Mackleby-Terra-looked nervously from Nina to Ken.

"If we all share access, it shows the togetherness of-"

"I can't agree to that," Sloane stated. She was surprised no one else was speaking up. She had important federal government access on her server. Although it would probably take a genius to figure out how to hack into any of it using a shared router, it wasn't safe to go around sharing passwords with random neighbors.

Rick, Ken, and Terra continued to sit, saying nothing.

"Let's table this," said Jackson. "Could we discuss the issue of parking? I know Leonardo had some comments about his space the other day, and-"

"There are no assigned spots," exclaimed Nina. "If Leonardo has a problem with parking, he can park near the construction vehicles. There is plenty of parking on that side of Sloane's duplex."

Jackson added, "It's just that when we bought the house, we were promised one spot in front of each of our houses, and if you have two vehicles, you should move one away from the front of your duplex so your neighbor can-"

Nina fumed. "Ken and I both need to access our vehicles quickly!"

Sloane wondered why Nina needed easy access to her stupid SUV. She didn't have kids or a job. Ken slunk further into the sofa and didn't even bat an eye.

Rick, who had been staring uncomfortably at a porcelain doll on Nina's side table, suddenly perked up and looked around the room as if seeing it all for the first time. "Say, why isn't Drew here?"

"He makes a good point," Sloane said. "Neither the Pacillis nor Drew are here. We should get their input on this stuff, especially security."

"Drew hasn't moved in yet and he's working late anyway," said Nina icily. "His shifts changed from morning to afternoon this week." Then, as though she felt she needed to rub it in that she had a communicative relationship with the officer, she added, "He tells me these things."

Sloane shrugged. She didn't care if they talked to each other. *Or do I,* she wondered. *I wonder what else they talk about when discussing me and my laundry?*

Jackson grew restless beside her. "Okay, so we have a *no* on laundry, a potential *yes* on rugs and plants though, something about internet, and zero restitution on the parking situation. Do I have that clear?"

Charlie glanced at her notes and muttered, "Yuh-huh, that's what I have."

Terra Mackleby leaned forward for cookie, somehow making Ken sink further into the middle of the sofa. "We should just follow the condo rules on everything."

"I thought we were trying to figure out what they were," said Sloane.

Nina huffed.

Charlie grinned and faked a cough.

Rick tried to be helpful by adding, "I'll try to make sure I park in the correct location in front of my house."

Mackleby chimed in again. "The front of your house is the only place we *can't* park. Mr. Stone's car is there and is still technically a crime scene."

Everyone turned to look at Jackson, save for Ken who was still nervously gawking at his lap. Jackson's face turned a deep crimson. He stood to leave, saying, "This meeting is ridiculous. We're not getting anything discussed. Why bother?"

Nina said, "We should talk about board positions."

Sloane faked a yawn. "I'm already in a bored position." She stood with Jackson.

Charlie offered her notes to Nina. "If they're going, so am I."

Rick and Terra stood as well, and both reached over Ken to shake each other's hand.

Nina attempted to make the end of the meeting her idea. "Okay, meeting adjourned at 7:37. Next time we'll see if the other neighbors are available," she said this toward Sloane, as though trying to insist there weren't any undertones. "And I'll come up with notes and suggested board positions."

Everyone muttered some random affirmative thought, and the group descended toward the door. Sloane grabbed the bowl of mostly uneaten cookies, put her sunglasses on, and tried to pretend like walking back outside wasn't the most terrifying idea on the planet. Nina held the door as Rick and Terra left together, chatting mindlessly about various pets they'd owned throughout the years. Charlie led the threesome out and Sloane ducked and followed her like a scared child, attempting not to display any of her obvious panic.

Jackson put his hand on Sloane's waist and followed the women out. Nina grabbed his shoulder and pulled him back, which startled Sloane and left her back exposed to the cool night air. The nerves in her spine began twitching, and her breath caught. Charlie noted it and turned to put her arm around

Sloane, so Sloane could dip her head into Charlie's shoulder. "We'd totally pass off as lesbians," whispered Charlie.

Sloane giggled, nervously, relieved at the helpful humor. They did not catch what Nina was whispering to Jackson.

Jackson caught up to them at the foot of the Smythe's steps, but never got close enough to touch Sloane again.

Sloane looked up at the Pacilli's house as they passed their porch, and she handed Jackson the bowl of cookies. "Could you bring these to Francesca? I feel bad that they weren't at the meeting."

Jackson took them and climbed the Pacilli's staircase. Charlie swept Sloane back into her house and shut the door, leaving it unlocked for Jackson.

Sloane collapsed onto her foyer floor and let her breathing return to normal. "That was horrible," she finally said. "I never want to go through that again."

"But hey," said Charlie. "You made a few good digs there, and you met the neighbors. I think it went well. Maybe at next month's meeting she'll declare you Chief of her Staff!"

"Shut up or I'll have you tossed in the dungeons," Sloane whined, then she crawled up the stairs on her hands and knees and headed straight for the wine cabinet.

CHAPTER TWENTY-TWO

Sloane carried a wine bottle to the living room and collapsed, Charlie took out three wine glasses and a corkscrew, and followed her to the couch. "That was a tough one, bestie, but you carried it off in spades!"

"Don't lie to me," Sloane laughed. "I was a total mess out there."

"Baby steps! Today, the house next door! Tomorrow, the world!"

They giggled at each other as Jackson came up the stairs and seated himself in the plush recliner across from them.

Charlie handed him a glass of wine. "What did Nina want?"

"She told me not to come to any more HOA meetings, since I'm under suspicion" Jackson made air quotes.

Sloane scowled. "She probably just wants fewer people there to defend my laundry honor! What a bitch. Speaking of people who weren't there, were the cookies delivered?"

"Cookies were delivered. They were definitely home. Leonardo said thank you, and Francesca started eating them right away. I think that baby is just about ready to burst out of her. She's huge!"

"Now now," Sloane condemned. "Never let a woman hear you calling her huge."

"Even if she's like ten months pregnant?"

"*Especially* if she's like ten months pregnant," Charlie mocked. "That's when they're at their most vulnerable!"

"Good to know. That explains why my ex-wife doesn't talk to me."

Sloane was suddenly interested in the conversation "you have a kid?"

"No, just an ex who mysteriously got pregnant while I was working in a different city."

Charlie and Sloane frowned. Charlie still had questions "She cheated on you but you stayed with her?"

"I'm a forgiving guy! Stuck it out for a few months and then called her huge. It didn't last long after that."

"Sounds like you're better off," said Charlie, and topped up her wine glass.

"Luckily it was amicable. There wasn't much to split and we hadn't been married long. I just saw her back in Kansas City last weekend. That's where I was, before - " Jackson didn't continue the thought. They all knew what he was referring to. Alanis's death.

Charlie still knew very little about Jackson. She asked, "Were you and Alanis -?"

"No," Sloane and Jackson both said simultaneously. Sloane blushed. Charlie smiled.

The room quieted as they stopped talking, presumably considering the horrible murder that had occurred mere days ago. Was that all the time that had passed? To Sloane, it seemed like an eternity. A long, unsolved eternity.

Charlie voiced out loud what Sloane was thinking. "I wonder if they've made any progress on solving that."

Jackson shrugged and looked at the floor. Sloane mused more to herself than to others, "It just seems so strange." *Why Jackson's roommate? Why in their cozy little community?* There was no explanation.

Clearly uncomfortable with the negativity inflicted on their otherwise fun evening, Charlie slightly changed the subject back to dating. With a sly wink to Sloane, she asked Jackson, "So, are you currently dating anyone?"

Jackson smiled, "Does spending my evening with you ladies count?"

Charlie giggled, in her enticingly bubbly way. Sloane rolled her eyes. "You wish. Charlie has a boy toy waiting for her at her bar."

A pink hue crossed Charlie's tan flesh. She smiled into her wine glass. As the three friends chatted about life, the universe and everything, Sloane felt her heartbeat slow and her breathing ease.

She mused aloud. "Future HOA meetings could benefit from alcohol."

"Amen to that!" said Jackson and raised his glass in a toast, before chugging the rest of his drink.

"I hate to bail," said Charlie. "But I should get back to my boy toy at the bar."

Charlie got up from the couch and looked back to Sloane. "If you're feeling better, babe, I'm out. I'll call you tomorrow, okay?"

Sloane wanted to hug her goodbye, but her legs were still slightly jellified. She mimed a hug into the air and said, "Love you."

Charlie gave Jackson a hug around the shoulders and descended the stairs.

Jackson's smile fell as she disappeared from sight, and he turned to Sloane. "Agoraphobia? Why did I not pick up on that?"

"I'm comfortable in my house, that's why. When you come to the door with my mail, I panic a little bit every time I hear the knock, but as long as I can stay on this side of the threshold, I'm generally okay. Inside another building, I'm okay, it's just-" she waved her hand toward the window, and beyond that toward the vast expanse of dark night sky. "Out there, I panic."

"Why is that? Tell me the story."

"It just happens to people sometimes," Sloane said. She did not want to start a conversation about seeing ghosts. First of all, Jackson probably wouldn't believe her, but on the tiny chance he did, he may ask too many questions about Alanis.

Alanis's business was her own, Sloane felt.

Sloane shook her head, using the opportunity to double check that they were apparition-less. "I'm so sorry, my psychoses is terrible."

"Hey, it's cool. I don't have a TV so I need some extra stories in my life."

"Truth is stranger than fiction, right?" Sloane relaxed her tense muscles. "You didn't know, it's fine. I go through this every once in a while with my therapist, and he frustrates me as well."

I also talk about it with a ghost, but somehow that's far less scary.

Sloane stood with her empty wine glass.

Jackson blew out an uncomfortable breath but said nothing. Instead, he collected his glass and the almost-empty wine bottle, and followed Sloane to the kitchen to help wash them.

"It's no bother," said Sloane, looking at the glasses. "I'll throw them in the dishwasher. You're fine."

"I - okay." Jackson gave a nervous smile. "I should hit the hay," he finally said. "Can I, uh, bring by some mail tomorrow?"

"Of course," smiled Sloane. Then, trying to ease the tension, added "I'm always here."

Jackson chuckled. "That, you are."

He retreated to the stairs. Sloane followed him to the door. "Thanks," she said as he walked out into the world.

"Thanks for what?"

"For this," she said, and gestured to the street and toward Nina Smythe's house. She hadn't been further than the mailbox or the next-door neighbor's house in weeks, and he had been a guiding force in that.

"Anytime." He turned and walked across the road. She closed the door and bolted it three times.

CHAPTER TWENTY-THREE

Alanis's ghost returned to the master bedroom that night, and although Sloane tried to ignore it, she found herself waking frequently just to check that the apparition was still there.

It didn't speak, just floated in the corner of Sloane's bedroom, watching her.

"Why aren't you talking," Sloane asked it.

No answer, more floating.

"Are you mad because I was talking to Jackson? Did he do this to you?"

No answer. The ghost seemed to flit between watching Sloane and looking out the window.

Sloane drifted in and out of slumber, willing the Pacillis to start their typical morning argument, or for Charlie to pop in for a rare morning visit, or even for Nina to pound on the door demanding that she remove her pillowcases from the balcony. Something, anything to get the ghost to stop stalking her.

"I can't solve this without your help," Sloane pleaded with the apparition.

At four in the morning, before the sun's ascent, she'd had enough of attempting to sleep like a normal human being.

Instead, she stood in a hot shower for thirty minutes willing the ghost to disappear when she came back out again.

She laughed despite herself, and let the hot water beat down on her face until it turned lukewarm. *I'm talking to a spirit like it's an annoying friend. It might not even be there. I might just have a mental disorder and be imagining it all!*

When she left her master bathroom, the ghost wasn't in the corner anymore. Sloane laughed again. *I am mad. I need a shrink not an exorcist.*

She threw on a thick robe and toddled downstairs to make herself some coffee.

Alanis' ghost was floating by the balcony door.

Sloane just laughed again, causing the ghost to stir. "I am going insane," Sloane cried, giggling.

Still early and dark, Sloane figured it would be a good time to bring in the laundry, lest Nina spot it and begin a tirade. She grabbed the basket by the dining room door, and peeked out into the cold, wary of the demons haunting both the outside and the inside of her house.

"I'm just going to step outside and get the laundry," she told the ghost. It stared at her, its haunting eyes mostly transparent now. "I don't know why I'm telling you this."

Because of the darkness, Sloane couldn't see much past the community gates. She slipped out onto the concrete, wincing at the chill on her bare feet, and began collecting her spoils. While the wind had dried her clothes overnight, a soft palette of dew cloaked them again. She decided the rest of the drying could be done by spreading them around the inside of her house. It wasn't worth a battle with Nina when she should be expecting a dryer from Drew sometime soon.

As she moved to the right side of the balcony, looking past the unoccupied unit in her duplex, she spotted a flickering light in the unfinished building. *Unusual*, she thought to herself, as she didn't think the electricity and fixtures had been installed yet. The outside of the building remained an empty shell of plywood and blue tarp. The window installers had been and gone, leaving it an empty carcass with beautiful and expensive dual panes.

"But it shouldn't be lit yet," she whispered out loud to the darkness. The light flickered out, and the unfinished building was dark and quiet once again. Behind it, the white Plymouth remained parked, guarding the neighborhood and its mysteries therein.

By six, the sun was up, and the small community began its whispered morning activity. Alanis's ghost remained silent, watching through the balcony sheers.

The Pacillis were arguing in dual languages again, a welcome sound for Sloane's lonely ears. Ken went for a walk around the neighborhood, as usual, and his busybody wife Nina watered her plants again. Rick took his tiny Dachshund into the neighboring forest. Sloane watched them all from her perch in the opposite corner from Alanis.

"I wish you'd talk to me again," she said. "I'd love to gossip about this."

"Gossip," the ghost seemed to echo, but Sloane didn't know if that was her own voice being repeated, or if Alanis's spirit could communicate at all anymore.

"Is it time for you to go?" Sloane asked. She had noticed the ghost's shape and form had grown more translucent by the day. *Perhaps the ghosts disappear over time, moving into the light or whatever.*

She'd never had a full conversation with one like she'd had with her dead neighbor. It was possible Alanis would be altogether gone very soon. Sloane felt guilty for not knowing how to help solve her murder.

Alanis' spirit seemed to focus on a point across the street, and Sloane followed its gaze.

Jackson's house remained closed and unlit, and nothing looked awry at all. The blinds in Alanis' old room remained closed.

Sloane shrugged and walked toward the kitchen to refill her coffee. "At some point I have to get back to government work," she said. "I can't watch the neighborhood all day, like some souls I know!"

She paced upstairs to the office and sat at her computer, preparing for the lengthy process of logging into various levels of government security. "Security shmecurity," she huffed. "So many passwords." She lived with nobody. Barely anyone came into her house except for her best friend and a lost ghost. "This is so pointless," she fumed, typing yet another different password into another government portal.

By lunchtime, she felt she'd worked hard and wanted to treat herself to some fresh air. She felt bold enough to test the balcony alone again.

Alanis' ghost had disappeared from the main level, which surprisingly shook Sloane's nerves a little. She'd started to enjoy knowing the ghost was there, watching from inside the window, in case something terrible happened outside.

Still, she'd have to get over her agoraphobia herself, in a reasonable way, at some point. She couldn't trust ghosts to solve her mental disorders.

Sloane sidled over to the balcony window, peering outside just to be sure no overwhelming neighbors, mainly Nina, were lurking nearby, then she eased herself out onto the patio and closed the door behind her, leaning on it for safety, but still peering out into the open air. Progress, albeit small.

The neighborhood was quiet, but not unusually so. Everyone would be at work by now, doing whatever it was they did, and even the construction team had softened their noises. Over the course of the last week, their hard hammering had dwindled to much more soothing sounds of fiberglass hauling and insulation. Perhaps the electricity was going in, after all, and the flickering light she'd seen earlier was merely a bulb left dangling in the airy plywood shell. The workers, mostly men in their early to mid-thirties, were a safe distance to be mere eye candy and not a threat.

A red car turned off the main road into the neighborhood, and Sloane's heart pummeled her chest in fear, before quickly abating. She recognized it as Drew Byrd's Ford again. As he passed, he looked up at Sloane, waved and pointed in the direction of his house. She hoped he did not intend for her to walk over there. She realized he was indicating the laundry machine he'd promised her, but she pretended she didn't read his cues and merely shrugged and waved hello.

I'm such a faker, she thought, *perhaps I'll have to explain my sordid story to him as well.*

Aloud, she whispered through her teeth as she waved, "I hope you don't need two people to lug that thing to my house."

If he does, I'll ask Jackson to help him out later. I'm sure they'll both love that.

She watched him pull up in front of his house and climb out of his car, the morning sunlight showing off his non-uniformed muscles. He was a handsome man, and fun to watch.

Nearby, a door opened. Sloane froze in panic, her heart racing. She looked behind herself through the glass of the balcony door, and, seeing nothing, looked to her left and right. Francesca Pacilli – actually, mostly her belly - was protruding out the door of their own balcony doors, only ten feet from Sloane's.

Sloane's shoulders fell, but she remained tense. The fact that the passageway between their houses was only a five-foot leap made her nervous, but she trusted Francesca and Leonardo and was glad that she got to call them her neighbors.

Francesca padded out onto her balcony with her eyes closed and faced the sun. She sucked in a breath of fresh air. Her hands entwined her belly and moved in a cyclical motion, massaging the infant within. She seemed to revel in the light, and Sloane didn't want to disturb her bliss by indicating that she was there. Instead, she stared in awe and wonder, moving her eyes from Francesca's blissful glow up into the sky towards the sun.

Apollo you are a fearsome, overwhelming necessity, Sloane thought, but she hoped one day she'd be well enough to bask in its light the same way her beautiful neighbor, a seeming goddess of fertility, did.

Sloane sighed, before she caught herself.

Francesca opened her eyes, "Miss Sloane!"

"Hello Francesca," Sloane's voice cracked. In slower, more enunciated words, she said, "you look beautiful," and gestured to Francesca's stomach.

Francesca looked down to her belly, smiled and nodded. Then her mouth formed an O-shape, and she held up an index finger to indicate that Sloane should wait. She ran inside her house, as fast as a nine-month pregnant woman might "run."

Sloane laughed, nervously.

A few seconds later, her neighbor toddled back out again, careful to hold herself and her precious cargo while stepping over the balcony threshold. In her right hand she carried the cookie bowls Sloane had sent over in the previous days.

In her left was a covered dish, which steamed in the crisp November air. Francesca fussed, looking at both hands, and chose to put down the steaming dish and try handing Sloane the bowl over their balcony railings.

Her belly did not let her lean very far, and Sloane moved toward the closest stretch of balcony. Shutting her eyes, she leaned over the chasm as far as she could too, to grab the cookie bowl.

They just barely made the handoff, and Francesca said, "Thank you" in accented English.

A touch of concern furrowed Francesca's brow, but she wiped it away, then rubbed her belly and licked her lips to translate the rest of the gratitude into a language Sloane understood. She had enjoyed the bounty.

Sloane was pleased and leaned back into the safety of her world.

Francesca held up a finger again and grabbed the steaming dish beside her. "Panzarotti," she said, drawing out the syllables. "Italian."

Sloane smiled and attempted thanks in Italian, "grazie?" But she had to take a deep breath and close her eyes again to retrieve the dish from Francesca.

Francesca blushed and grinned ear to ear. "Thank you," she said again, obviously flattered that Sloane had attempted to communicate, but without words to express her feelings.

Sloane bowed her head quick and awkwardly, and stepped back toward her balcony door, heart racing.

Francesca took another breath of fresh air, laughed, and retreated inside.

The scent of pasta and vegetables consumed Sloane's senses, and she too escaped to her dining room to enjoy the fresh lunch, taking one last look up at the sun as a show of defiance toward the evil it had bestowed upon her.

Look, sky, I can go out for Italian food; from right next door.

#

Halfway through her second to last panzarotti, she heard the locks on the door ping with jangling keys, the calling card of Charlie. As her best friend swallowed the staircase two at a time, Sloane called from the dining table, "Why don't you just move in with me? You don't even knock anymore."

"Too late, babe. Darius asked me to move in with him." Charlie rounded the top of the stairs and smiled at her friend, then eyed the remaining panzarotti. She didn't bother asking before she grabbed and began devouring it.

"No massage clients today?" Sloane asked, more disgruntled at the loss of her lunch than curious about why Charlie was there on a weekday. She walked to the coffee machine to start running it. She knew Charlie must be stopping in before the dinner shift at the bar.

"Nah, business is still slow, as usual," Charlie hummed. "Faith is teaching me how to read tarot cards, now that her side of the business is picking up, she wants me to join the action."

"Nice, that's decent money."

"It is, but some of her clientele are a little… well, you know." Charlie spun a finger around her ear.

"You seem to attract a lot of us 'you knows'" Sloane repeated the action.

"Speaking of that, how are you doing?"

"Not bad, actually. I went out on the balcony alone twice today."

Sloane told her about the lack of sleep but left out Alanis' ghost. She talked about getting Francesca's delicious Italian snacks but didn't mention that she'd leaned across a 15-foot drop to retrieve them from the balcony.

Charlie seemed to sense it was a stressful event, though. She shook her head. "Want me to stay here after work tonight? We could have a good old-fashioned sleepover and watch girly movies."

"I'd like that, yes." Sloane smiled again.

The two grabbed another mug of coffee, and Charlie gestured to the balcony. "I need some fresh air before spending the night at the bar. Let's people watch."

Sloane was comfortable enough with her friend there that she led the way.

"Hey, look at you," grinned Charlie. "Walking outside in front of me. Want to make this a party with some wine?"

"Nah, I have more work to do this afternoon and I shouldn't be drunk if Drew is bringing that dryer over today."

"He's not expecting you to go over and help, is he?"

"I hope not." She looked toward Drew's house. His car was still out front, but she didn't see any movement.

A car turned into the neighborhood, one Sloane seemed to recognize from somewhere, but she didn't know where. It moved slowly past her house, and the tinted windows hid the face of whoever was driving.

"Who is that?" inquired Charlie.

"I don't know. I've never seen them before. Perhaps house shoppers."

"Oh, maybe they'll move in next door!"

Sloane's skin prickled under her robe. She didn't like the idea of brand-new neighbors sharing a wall with her. She was happy knowing an empty void existed next door, and she was comfortable with the passionate but friendly Pacilli's on the other side of the alley. She didn't want to meet anyone new.

The car slowed and pulled up in front of Principal Mackleby's house.

"Ah," said Sloane, "they're parking in front of the empty home next to Terra. Yeah, they must be shoppers."

"Hmm," muttered Charlie, "it's a weird car for a townhome buyer. Tinted windows and a Bentley? That's a bit fancy for our usual resident."

"It *is* weird, that's for sure, but you never know. People do funny things. Maybe it's another newly divorced person and they wanted to get as far away from a bougie mansion that they lost to the ex."

The friends watched the car, but no one got out or in. It sat there, engine running.

"Listening to the radio, maybe?" wondered Charlie.

"Spying on someone?" mused Sloane.

"Oh. Maybe it's related to Alanis's death. It's the killer come back for more!"

"Don't say that" hushed Sloane. "Besides, that car wasn't in the neighborhood when Alanis died. Unless the killer had parked on the highway and traipsed in through the woods, I would have spotted them."

"So keenly aware, you are, for having never gone outside."

"I'm outside right now!" She tapped her friend on the arm, but a side of her was still questioning the presence of the automobile. Who was sitting there, and who were they watching? She shuddered at the thought.

"Okay babe, I'm leaving for work. This person is too weird even for me," said Charlie, but she chuckled as she said it, to indicate that she was kidding about the spookiness factor. Sloane followed her inside. "I'll be back later. Stay alive, okay?"

"You bet. Just me and my number crunching machine for the rest of the day. And a new dryer, if I can get one."

They hugged, and Sloane followed her down to the door, keeping an eye out the windows on that interesting black Bentley.

Still no movement, even after Charlie had left.

CHAPTER TWENTY-FOUR

When Sloane climbed back upstairs to get back to work, Alanis' ghost hovered in a corner of the office, looking out a side window toward the Pacilli's house.

"See anything interesting," Sloane asked. All of her fear was gone now. Alanis felt more like a roommate than a haunt. It was devastating what had happened to her, and Sloane wished she'd tell her more about her life.

As it was, it didn't seem like anyone missed her that much. Jackson had mentioned she was in a difficult situation when she moved in, maybe it was serious.

The ghost said nothing, so Sloane sat down at her desk and logged into work. As she toiled away at boring network stuff, her mind and eyes kept flittering out the front window to the car in the street. Sloane hadn't seen anyone get out or in since Charlie left.

"Do you know that person," Sloane asked the ghost.

Alanis seemed to float toward Sloane and the window. The hairs on Sloane's arm prickled a bit at the approaching apparition, but she calmed herself with deep breathing. She was safe. Besides feeling icky when she'd ran into it before, it wasn't clear if the ghost could affect anything around it. But even if it could, it hadn't tried anything yet.

It said nothing, but it almost appeared as though it had shaken its head.

"Why could you talk before, but you can't now?"

Alanis began to disappear.

"Time is running out, huh?"

Alanis was almost gone.

"I wish I could help you, I really do," Sloane said quickly, flustered. *Am I going to miss her when she's gone for good?* "I don't know what to do."

Alanis was gone. Sloane dared to step over to where the apparition last appeared, but besides a chill from perhaps moving too quickly, she sensed nothing. She looked out the window, the car was still there. Nina was out on her porch watering her plants again.

Sloane wandered downstairs and spoke to the coffee machine. "I can't work in these conditions. There needs to be a mandatory government vacation for 'there was a murder across the street, and I feel responsible.'"

She wished Alanis would come back so that at least she wasn't kidding around with inanimate objects.

A knock rattled the door. Sloane's skin crawled and her mouth dropped open in shallow breaths. She hoped it was someone she knew, and not a mysterious Bentley driver who had sat for no reason for so long.

Her hopes were met when Drew Byrd stood at her door, with a dolly carrying a dryer. He'd obviously toiled a bit with it, as a vee of sweat darkened the shirt by his muscular pecs. Sloane tried not to stare.

"Appliance delivery!" He cheered when she widened the door frame.

Before she let him in, she dared to peek out the door at the Bentley up the road. The engine looked to be off, but she felt the driver was still in there. She had a strong sense of it. He or she wouldn't have gone into the model home for a three-hour tour, would they?

Drew set the dolly down and followed her gaze up the street. "Someone bothering you there, ma'am? Detective Byrd is on the case!"

Sloane's tension relaxed and she smiled. "It's fine. Just a strange car in the neighborhood, that's all. I don't like strangers."

"I hope you don't consider me a stranger, I come bearing gifts." Drew turned back from the car toward Sloane, and he nodded as if to ask, 'Can I come in?'

"Oh, sorry, where are my manners?" Sloane ignored the Bentley and shut the door behind Drew. Together, they went step by step up the two flights to the laundry room. Drew seemed to have no problem with the dolly, thanks to his large muscles. As she steadied the machine from below, Sloane couldn't help but grab subtle looks at the definition of his triceps.

No harm in looking, right Alanis?

She wished Alanis was there. Or Charlie. Or anyone who would enjoy this view with her.

As Drew neared the top of the second staircase, it was apparent the weight of the machine had gotten to him. He grunted heavily. "Why the hell did the builders have to put these laundry machines up three flights? You've got plenty of space in that empty downstairs room."

Sloane froze for a brief second. Had he been in her house?

It took her a moment to realize she'd let him into the downstairs room only a few days ago, to show him where the blood was. Her shoulders relaxed.

"True," she said, half laughing and half nervous. "Although who wants to descend two full flights to do laundry in the morning? Especially when I have to haul it back up to hang it on the balcony."

"No more balcony hanging!" Drew raised his arm and flexed a muscle, "I've saved the day again."

"You really have. By the way, how can I thank you for this? It saves me a ton of harassment from Nina Smythe."

Drew smiled. "No thanks necessary. Also, I think you ought to give her a break. She has a lot of stuff going on right now."

Sloane felt a twinge of embarrassment, but it disappeared just as quickly. "Does she, though? She stays at home and has no kids." Sloane quickly added a disclaimer, "Not that housewives don't have business to take care of, of course!"

"But," she added, "Nina seems to water her plants and get in my hair. That's all I know about her."

"Well," thought Drew, and he ultimately shook his head too. "I don't know either, but she comes up to me a lot asking for help with random things around her house. It seems her fridge or internet or floorboard is always breaking."

"Ah," said Sloane. "Sounds more like she's trying to hit on you."

"No! She's married!" Drew paused by the small laundry closet, preparing to pull out the broken machine. Then he scratched his head. "You think?"

"I know. That's the kind of behavior we all do when we need a strong man to come help us out," Sloane blushed.

"Like when you need us to lend you a dryer and haul it up your stairs?"

"Hey," Sloane's cheeks reddened further. "You offered this to me, remember?" Then she eased her tone and chuckled. "Again, thank you so much for this."

After Drew and Sloane got the machine installed and the broken one back onto the dolly to be brought downstairs, Sloane asked, "Would you like a drink? Coffee? Beer?"

"I'm on duty later this afternoon." Drew thought about it. "So yes, I'd love a beer."

They descended to the kitchen slowly, Sloane guiding the front of the dolly. As Drew moved toward the last flight of stairs, Sloane grabbed two Schlafly ales out of the fridge. She popped the caps off with a butter knife from the counter.

Drew caught this act. "Woah, opening a bottle with whatever is lying around? You're skilled in the art of beer." He began his last descent and she followed with the beers.

"A natural talent for those of us who lose our belongings during moves. One must be able to open sustenance with whatever tool is available."

"Haven't mastered opening a beer with the forehead or teeth yet, have you?" He joked.

"Not yet. I need to preserve my forehead for scowling at the neighbors when I'm old."

Drew's eyes widened as he descended into the front foyer. "Woah. You're scary. I like that."

Sloane led them out onto the porch, where Drew brought the old dryer down the final steps and set it on the curb. Sloane was glad that holding a beer in each hand prevented her from needing an excuse for not leaving her front doorway to help with the dryer the rest of the way.

"Thanks again for the dryer," she attempted to say but he returned and waved a hand to cut her off. He took a cold beer from her hand.

"You've said thanks a hundred times already, and you did most of the installing! I'm really no gentleman." He chugged the beer, clearly exhausted but hiding it well. A bead of sweat rolled down his muscular collar bone.

Sloane laughed. She did enjoy some conversations with the living, especially handsome living people. They sat together on the front steps, and she did her best to disguise her fear by taking deep glugs of her bee rand leaning into him.

He did not protest.

Sloane didn't know whether to ask him more questions about himself or let him fidget with his own thoughts. She chose the latter herself, staring at the black car still sitting outside the empty townhome. She couldn't spot the driver, but she knew he was there. She had a feeling. Her body shivered.

"Cold?" Drew was concerned.

"No, I just - There's this guy sitting in a strange car over there, and he's been there for a few hours, and it's starting to freak me out a little bit." As she gestured towards the car and Drew's view followed her hand, the engine of the Bentley roared to life, and the car crept out of the neighborhood, taking the small access road next to Rick's house. It wasn't a real street, just an old construction path from when the houses went up. Sloane shivered again.

"Strange," said Drew. "I can look into it if you want. Maybe he's the realtor manning a model home?"

"I don't think so," said Sloane. "He never left his car to do anything."

Drew shrugged and stared out into the forest at the end of the lane, as though looking for something.

They sipped their beer in silence.

CHAPTER TWENTY-FIVE

Jackson arrived home as Drew was leaving Sloane's house. He took his time exiting his vehicle, awkwardly shifting his gaze from his car to the two of them.

When Drew turned away from Sloane and spotted him, Jackson seemed to give him a nervous wave, then headed toward his house. Drew glared at him, said goodbye to Sloane, and headed in the direction of his own townhome.

Sloane, feeling emboldened, raced to the mailboxes by the curb. She kept them in focus and tried to block out the overwhelming outdoor world.

She jumped when Jackson strode up beside her. "Any mail for me?"

She unlocked her mailbox and it all but overflowed again. As she scrambled to collect it all, she smirked. "Were you waiting for the good detective to leave before you came over here to say hi?"

"Wouldn't you?" Jackson questioned her. "That man is currently investigating me for murder."

Sloane laughed, flipping through her mail and handing Jackson an envelope with his name on it. She tried to stand back while he opened his own mailbox, but she needed his body to shield her from the vast, terrifying sky above. "You can't be uncivil to Drew, Jackson, he'll think you're guilty."

"Hey, you saw me wave at him."

Sloane rolled her eyes and gestured for him to come in and visit. The outside was now really starting to speed up her heart.

Or is it the handsome man beside me? Or the one who just left? Her brain asked her these questions before she could squash the emotion. She could *not* have a relationship in her current state, especially not with two different men.

"Inviting in two handsome guys in one afternoon? You get around," Jackson laughed as though reading her mind. But there was a not-so-subtle hint of jealousy to his tone.

"You think pretty highly of yourself, Mr. Stone."

"Nah, I just think pretty lousy of *him*." Jackson drew out the last syllable and scrunched his face. Sloane closed her door behind him and they both started rifling through their mail.

"Don't pout, silly boy, or I won't invite you in again."

"I probably shouldn't be here anyway, what with Officer Bigman requesting I be on house arrest."

Sloane shook her head at his ridiculous insult.

"Have I ever told you what I do?" he asked her.

"Sure, you work for the state government. You write software or whatever."

"Yes, but-" Jackson lowered his voice. Sloane wondered who he thought would be listening. "Yes, but no. My specific computer systems are used in all sorts of government levels, from city through to the feds."

"Okay," Sloane didn't have any idea where this conversation was going or what it had to do with her, but goosebumps formed on her arm.

"So, one of my clients is the federal government."

"Oh! That's fun." Sloane continued looking through her giant stack of mail, but she wasn't focusing on the names anymore. She started to feel a bit nervous.

"Anyway," Jackson tried to get her attention. "I figured out that you work there, too. I hope you're not upset."

Sloane chuckled, nervously. She put her mail down on the front hall table. "Is that all? You looked me up?" Her breathing became labored, but she tried to quash it down.

Jackson spotted it and stepped toward the door. "Sorry for snooping. I should go. I didn't see anything, just noticed your name in the system is all."

"Oh okay, cool," she eased her breath, but opened the door for him as well. She stood behind it so the outside world wouldn't get in.

"Hey, I'm sorry if I startled you. I just thought it was neat that we worked in similar fields." Jackson was genuinely apologetic.

Sloane scoffed and waved a hand at him. "No worries. No worries."

He stepped out onto her porch. "So, what do you do there, by the way? I told you I'm a software developer, what about you?"

"Oh, nothing exciting like that. Just administrative stuff, you know how it is."

"Ah, the boring stuff. Gotcha." He pointed gun fingers at her, which felt a little strange. "It's weird, though."

"What is," she breathed, willing him to leave.

"Your clearance level is so frickin' high, just for an admin."

"Oh, that-" Sloane laughed, nervously. "Yeah, well someone has to answer the White House emails, you know? Nobody over there seems to bother with them."

She wasn't sure why she felt she had to lie. Her job really wasn't that important. She just relayed messages from field agents to the head office, that's all.

Jackson nodded and turned toward his house. "Catch you later?" he called back to her.

"Catch you later," she half-whispered, shutting the door on him and everything else.

Why did that feel so weird?

"Software," a voice echoed from behind her. Sloane jumped.

Alanis's ghost hovered by the door to the empty first floor room.

"How long have you been standing there?" Sloane admonished the apparition, then thought herself quite silly for doing so.

"Software," the ghost replied.

"Yes, we both work in software. For the feds. It doesn't mean anything," Sloane stormed upstairs. *Does it?*

At the top of the stairs, she jumped out of her skin. Alanis was already on the main level, staring out the balcony window. Sloane looked back down the stairs and then again at the apparition. "Jesus, you've never done *that* before."

"I've never done what before," called Charlie from the front door.

"Christ!" Sloane screeched. There were too many people to talk to now, and life was becoming overwhelming again.

Alanis's ghost vanished.

Charlie breached the top step and hugged Sloane from behind. "Who are you talking to, babe? You seem tense."

"Why didn't I see you before? You've got to knock sometimes, babe."

"I happened to hear you and your handsome neighbor together, so I thought I'd hide out in the alley until he left, just in case you needed some time together."

Sloane was glad Charlie hadn't seen the previous handsome neighbor as well, or else she'd give Sloane a hard time about "dating" two men.

"I had other things on my mind," Sloane muttered. *Like crushes on all the neighbors and a ghost who now seems strangely obsessed with software development.*

"Oh, I can tell. I saw dreamy neighbor leave your house, and I can see the old dryer on your curb, which means handsome officer was here at some point, too." Charlie went to the wine cabinet and helped herself to a bottle and two glasses. She pointed Sloane in the direction of the balcony. "Those lounge chairs, and your gossip, await!"

CHAPTER TWENTY-SIX

The neighbors' voices woke her up again the next morning. Light arguing in mixed English wafted up on the wind through the alley. Sloane heard words like "I know" and "one week," but it was all she understood.

Sloane's tired mind started creating fantastical stories of what the couple next door might be fighting about. Perhaps the baby was one week overdue. Perhaps Leonardo was going on a one-week business trip and Francesca was even more upset than usual. Sloane crawled out of bed, donned her robe, and padded downstairs. It was still too early for work, so she opted to bake cookies again.

The voices carried on. Sloane couldn't solve their marriage problem, or their baby problem, but she could bake cookies and she knew they'd be appreciated. She hoped Francesca would come out on the balcony again so she could hand them over the iron railing again.

An hour after baking, she found herself outside on the balcony with a cup of coffee, the cookies cooling quickly on the chair Charlie had been in the night before. She fantasized about building some sort of trolley system to the Pacilli's house next door, then she laughed and shook her head at herself, thinking how ridiculous and pathetic it was that she could barely carry a plate of cookies next door by herself. She didn't need friends that badly.

Or did she?

She was seeing ghosts, after all. Perhaps it was her brain's cry for help.

Nina caught her off guard by yelling across the Pacilli's balcony. "No laundry today, I see."

Sloane startled and frowned. She plastered a fake smile on her face and replied, "Officer Drew set up the dryer for me yesterday, he was so sweet." That last part was said passive aggressively, just to watch an envious frown peel across Nina's face.

Nina righted her shoulders, clearly having nothing further to say on the subject. She turned to gossip instead, "Did he bring any word on the murder?"

"No." Sloane's tone changed as well, as she thought of poor helpless Alanis, wandering home late at night the previous weekend, not knowing what was to befall her.

"Well, hopefully they'll catch the perp soon," said Nina, "So the rest of us women aren't fearing for our lives." She tiled her head toward Jackson's door.

Now it was Sloane's turn to frown. *Tit for tat*, she supposed. "I don't think we're at risk, do you? It seems to be an isolated incident."

"Is it, though?" Nina shrugged and refocused on her plants.

Sloane was glad the conversation was over. Talking to Nina was enough outside world for her. It was clear Francesca was not going to come out anytime soon, so she stood to pick up her cookies and walk back inside.

Nina called after her, "Hey, by the way, did you see a strange car yesterday?"

Now Sloane was interested. "I did, actually. You're talking about the Bentley? Any idea whose it is?"

"Yes, I think it's a realtor," Nina insisted.

"If you'd spotted it, I would have thought you'd march right over there to find out who was in the car."

Nina missed the dig in the statement and took it as a complement instead. "Normally I would, but I was so busy yesterday I didn't think of it until it was gone. I called the developers later though. It's fine."

Sloane rolled her eyes. "Of course you did."

"Anyway, all good. I hope we get some new neighbors soon, don't you?"

"Yeah me too. I'll be sure to invite them to the HOA meeting." Sloane left and took herself inside, not waiting for a response from her nosiest neighbor.

CHAPTER TWENTY-SEVEN

"This was the thing about you," Sloane began, even before Alanis's ghost had fully formed. "You moved in right after me, right?"

Alanis floated inside the balcony window, watching Jackson's house. It said nothing.

Sloane continued, casually munching a cookie over the breakfast counter. "So, you were just some cousin of Jackson's who needed a room, right?"

Alanis slowly turned. Sloane felt no fear at all.

"But you look similar to me."

"Similar," the ghost repeated.

"I mean, you're more gorgeous. You have—had--bigger boobs, but your haircut and the shoulders, you could look like me. Do you think?"

Alanis' ghost stared at her.

Sloane looked into her empty coffee mug, and realized she was probably being ridiculous. "No. No, there is no reason to kill me. So why would there be a reason to mistake you for me? I think this whole situation is just starting to mess with me. And now Nina is talking about more new neighbors to scare the living daylights out of me."

"Nina," Alanis's voice echoed.

"Yeah, she's a nosy bitch, am I right?"

Alanis began to disappear again.

"Hey, I'm sorry. Don't leave--"

But it was too late, Alanis was gone. Sloane, typically an introvert, found herself missing the company.

She grabbed cookies and an empty dish and walked downstairs. Her locked door loomed in front of her, and as she twisted each of the three bolts, her heart pounded up through her ears and into her skull. She began to grow faint and dizzy, and as she stepped out onto the front porch, she almost vomited. The coast was clear, for now. She drew as much oxygen as she could into her faltering lungs, and plummeted into the vortex of the outside world, heading to the one door she trusted completely.

Luckily, Francesca was right by her own front door. After two hasty knocks, the door swung open to her full frame. Vibrant and comforting smells of pasta and fresh bread furled through Sloane's senses and she all but stumbled into their house. Francesca looked surprised, but stepped backwards and shut the door behind Sloane, as if she knew Sloane's affliction and was closing her off from the outside world.

Sloane leaned against the front hall wall and said, "thank you." She held up the box of cookies and the empty dish that once held panzerottis.

Francesca squealed and said, "come, come," waving her up the stairs to her main level, the reverse of Sloane's floorplan. "Sit, per favore." She fussed over a blanket on a lush, velvet sofa in her living room.

"It must be hard, not having many friends," Sloane said this mostly to herself, guessing Francesca might not understand what she was saying.

"Friend," Francesca smiled, pointing to Sloane. Then she went to her kitchen island and pulled out a plate.

"Yes, friend," Sloane agreed. She was glad she had proof of another friend. Charlie and her next therapist could suck it. *I have other living friends!*

Francesca brought the plate to the living room and set the cookies out on it. Then, she went back to her kitchen and fussed over a tea kettle. Once it was brewed, she brought it and two cups out on a tray.

Sloane took the empty cookie tray and set it beside herself, indicating that she would take it home after.

"Oh, you help me?" Francesca stated, appearing like she'd just remembered something. She held up a finger as if asking Sloane to wait.

"You need help with something?"

"Internet," Francesca said. She went to the dining room and grabbed a laptop.

When she walked back to the living room, she showed Sloane the laptop and said, "no internet."

"Ugh, don't tell me Nina's stupid plan is already in action," Sloane muttered to herself. Francesca looked at her helplessly. "Let me see what I can do." Sloane fidgeted with the laptop, clicking the Wi-Fi icon in the corner. "Is this your router? Pac1971?"

Francesca beamed. "Yes, yes! Password is FranLeoItalia."

As Sloane tried to figure out what was wrong with Francesca's connection, Francesca poured the tea and bent to sit in the chair across from Sloane. As she did so, she clutched her belly and groaned.

"Okay?" Sloane worried.

"Okay," smiled Francesca, still grinning but clearly in discomfort.

"You probably just need to reboot and run some updates on this old thing," Sloane restarted the laptop. As she did, she pointed to Francesca's belly and said "Name?"

Francesca's face brightened in understanding, but she blushed. "Leonardo and I, we fight about baby name." She spoke slowly to enunciate her English.

Sloane smiled. *That explained their harmless bickering.*

The laptop stirred to life and everything seemed in order. "Looks like you're online again," Sloane opened a browser.

Francesca squealed. "Thank you, Miss Sloane."

"I really didn't do much," Sloane shrugged. "But happy to help."

Francesca reached for a cookie then squeezed her belly and winced again.

"Problem?"

Francesca shook her head, but it was quite clear there was a problem. Sloane hoped she wasn't hiding anything from her, but realized the poor woman must be desperate for company while Leonardo was at work.

"Thank you for this, it's lovely," Sloane went to grab the teacup to indicate what she was talking about. As she did so, Francesca's leg hit the other side of the coffee table, and Sloane spilled the tea onto the coffee table.

Francesca gasped, "oh, so sorry!" and hastily stood up. As she did so, drops of fluid ran down her leg from beneath her skirt, and dripped onto her hardwood floor. She clutched her belly and groaned.

Sloane gasped, "Francesca, it's happening." She bounced up from her position, angled herself around the coffee table, and held Francesca by the shoulders, easing her onto the sofa instead of the chair.

Sloane tore her eyes around the room looking for a phone, wishing she'd brought her mobile over. "Phone?" Sloane held her thumb and pinky to her ear, hoping the sign for cellphone was universal. Francesca pointed toward the dining room wall, where an older phone was connected by wire. Almost unfamiliar in modern times, Sloane wondered if it was just cheaper for making long distance calls back to their homeland. She grabbed it off the wall and listened for a dial tone.

The ancient cord did not stretch all the way to the living room, so Sloane held it up and hoped Francesca understood enough to communicate, "Number?"

Francesca furrowed her brow attempting to come up with the proper English translation but couldn't do it. She held up fingers instead, one at a time.

Finally, Sloane connected to Leonardo's direct line at work.

A knock sounded at the door. Sloane's eyes grew wide and her heart stammered in her chest. Francesca tilted her body up and looked toward the stairs, then to Sloane. Sloane shrugged. This was no time for telemarketers or whoever was down there.

"Francesca?" Leonardo said through the other line, having recognized the number and assuming it was his wife.

Sloane whispered, "Leonardo, it's Sloane Jackson."

"Sloane Jackson? A surprise!" Leonardo seemed puzzled but pleased.

"Leonardo, your wife is in labor. Her water has broken, and it doesn't look good. Should I drive her somewhere to meet you?" She hoped the answer was no. She couldn't see herself going outside, even in an emergency. Also, she didn't have a car.

The knock on the door sounded again. "Mrs. Pacilli?" They heard Nina through the door, "just a friendly neighborhood visit!"

Nina? What the hell could she possibly want right now?

Sloane shook her head. Francesca nodded, clutching her belly and stifling a groan.

Leonardo was saying something, "-five minutes away and leaving now. I call when I'm there!" He trailed off as though taking the phone away from his ear. Sloane listened but the line went dead.

She raced across the room to try and ease Francesca's pain. "Do you have a baby bag?" she mimed holding a handle with her hands. Francesca nodded and pointed her hand toward the upper floor. Sloane went upstairs and found a small satchel near the bedroom. On the way back through the kitchen, she grabbed a dish towel as well. She wiped the liquid off the floor, now drying to a spotted black stain. As Francesca stood, Sloane wiped her legs for her, and gave her the towel. She also grabbed a pillow off the couch and held it out for Francesca, gesturing that she should hold it under her belly. The woman grabbed it and nodded her thanks, then they waited.

Sloane counted the minutes between contractions, and hoped the dark liquid didn't mean it was too late. It felt like an eternity until the phone rang again, then she helped the woman walk down the stairs. As they neared the door, Sloane eased a jacket for Francesca out of her closet. Sloane dared to open the door and peer out between the crack. Nina was long gone.

As Leonardo's car pulled in front of the house, Sloane widened the door and followed Francesca out. As long as she was staring at Francesca's back and holding on to her, she felt less exposed to the outside world.

Out of the corner of her eye, Sloane caught Jose rushing down Sloane's front steps.

"What are you doing at my house, Jose?"

Leonardo double parked the car and ran toward them to grab Francesca's hands. Both he and Francesca didn't seem to notice the commotion.

Jose seemed hurried, "Miss Sloane, I'm so sorry, I thought I heard something in your house, and I worried that you weren't there!"

Sloane couldn't think straight. She helped Leonardo get Francesca into the back of the car.

From behind her, she heard another familiar voice. "So you are there, you two," Nina called, although not from her front porch, she appeared to have come around from the back of the Pacilli's house. "I was trying to find you to invite you to the next HOA meeting. Nobody answered Francesca's door."

"We were a little busy," Sloane muttered, trying to avoid involving Nina in any of their business. She was beginning to feel completely overwhelmed by the number of people and the outside world.

Francesca groaned and Leonardo's face fell.

"She needs to get there soon. I think something is wrong," Sloane said to him.

He didn't stop to ask questions, he leapt into the driver's seat and peeled out of the neighborhood, as fast as a hybrid car can peel.

It took a moment for Sloane to realize she was exposed, helpless, alone but not.

She could hear both Jose and Nina talking at her, but her mind was starting to spin in circles. She bumped shoulders with the woman as she raced up her staircase. Nina seemed to be lingering between their two duplexes.

"Sorry," she muttered as Jose passed her. She ran into the house, shutting the door behind her and collapsing onto the floor.

It took her a moment to catch her breath, and then a puzzling thought occurred to her. Had she left her door wide open when she left with the cookies? Did Jose go all the way *inside* her house?

CHAPTER TWENTY-EIGHT

Sloane closed and locked the door, then crept up the stairs. Alanis's ghost was weak and transparent, but it hovered by the balcony door.

"Did someone come in here?" Sloane asked.

"Come in here," the ghost echoed.

"I don't know if you're saying yes or just repeating me anymore," Sloane scoffed. Time was clearly running out for Alanis. *What happens to spirits when their murder is never solved*, she wondered. *Will it just hover in the neighborhood for the rest of eternity? Is that what happened to all those old ghosts who moved between rooms in ancient houses? Did they also talk to the living?*

Sloane's main level looked otherwise in order, but she still felt something was off. A breeze carried up the stairs and tickled her neck.

I shut and locked the door just now, though. Didn't I?

She retraced her steps, halfway down the stairs. The front door was indeed locked.

"I'm imagining things," she said aloud as she went back up to the kitchen. "I think I'm just overwhelmed."

"Nina," Alanis's ghost echoed.

"Is that goddamn woman still standing out there?" Sloane approached the balcony window and peered through the sheers. She felt a chill from Alanis's ghost next to her, but it was more welcoming than creepy.

Nina was pretending to water her plants again, while spying on the neighborhood.

"She'll never give up, will she."

The ghost said nothing.

Again, a breeze seemed to tickle the hairs on Sloane's neck.

"Where is that breeze coming from?" She turned to ask the ghost, but it had all but disappeared.

Sloane shrugged and went upstairs to her office.

The window in her office was open.

Strange, she said to herself. *Did I open this when I was looking at the Bentley with Alanis?* She closed it.

The items on her desk seemed slightly out of place. She shook her mouse to awaken the computer screen. On it was a blue screen saying, 'Password Attempted Too Many Times.'

"Fuck. What the hell?"

She stared at the now-closed window.

This is impossible, she thought. *Nobody would have climbed up to a third-floor window and tried my password. Did Jose come in and upstairs this far? Did* he *do it?*

But Jose was a friend, it didn't make sense.

She started down the stairs. She'd have to call her IT department to unlock the computer. "I know my government access is important, but this is ridiculous. Can a simple breeze try a password too many times?"

Alanis was gone.

"Now I'm talking to myself. Great."

She dialed IT and left a message. Then she called Officer Byrd.

CHAPTER TWENTY-NINE

"I'm sure it's nothing," she repeated to him. The two of them stood in her office, looking for anything else that was out of place.

"Could it have been the breeze?" Drew wondered.

"I wondered that as well," Sloane shrugged. "That's a pretty intelligent breeze to try a password several times, though."

"Tell me what you saw when you left Francesca's house." Drew had a notebook out.

"It wasn't Jose," Sloane insisted. "I trust him. I'm sure of it. I just called you over because--in case something fishy happens--there needs to be a police report so I'm not fired."

"I get it, I get it, just explain the series of events," he insisted.

Sloane described the timeline from baking the cookies to putting Francesca in her car to going upstairs to check on things. Again, she left out the ghost.

\#

After taking his notes, Officer Byrd looked around Sloane's upper floors. They ended up on the balcony, and shortly thereafter Nina appeared on her front porch, again.

"Hello Officer Byrd," she smiled. "What are you doing up there?"

Drew waved at her. Sloane ignored her neighbor, opting instead to wander toward the unfinished duplex next to hers. She wondered when it might be completed.

Sloane overheard Nina say something to the effect of, "You shouldn't be socializing while there is an investigation going on, officer." Then she heard Nina's door close.

Sloane turned to Drew, "What's her problem with you?"

"I'm not sure," said Drew. "Sometimes I think she has a bizarre little crush on me, and sometimes I just think she's obsessed with finding the murderer."

Sloane laughed, "Could be both."

"Married women are not my type."

"I sometimes wonder if they're legit married, I've barely seen them talk to each other."

Drew shrugged.

"What *is* your type?" Sloane said without thinking, then blushed.

"Dryerless women, obviously!" Now it was his turn to blush.

"Flirting on the job, now that's something you definitely shouldn't be doing while an investigation is going on, *officer*."

Drew laughed at her mockery of Nina. But as they stepped back inside her house, he turned serious. "Tell me what your relationship is with Jackson."

Sloane stopped, and Drew almost crashed into her. She turned toward him. "Now wait a minute here, Byrd. Am I back under investigation? Will my words be used against him?"

"They may be."

She huffed and went toward the staircase down to the front door. "I appreciate your honesty, Officer Byrd. There is nothing going on between me and Mr. Stone. We're neighbors and we enjoy each other's company. Now, if you don't mind. I have to get back into my computer." She held her hand over the stairs.

Drew passed by her. As he did, he stared into her eyes. It was disconcerting, but she held strong.

"Just be careful Sloane, alright? Until we know what happened to Alanis, we can't trust anyone who knew her."

She followed him down the staircase to the front door. "So that's why this investigation is stalled then, hmm? The fact is, hardly anyone knew her. Jackson himself barely knew her."

Drew nodded, sighed, and left the house. "Always lock your door behind guests!"

"I always do," she said and closed the door. She bolted it three times, clicking the locks as loudly as possible. He'd frustrated her, and she wondered if she was mad on behalf of Jackson, or because she held slight feelings for both of them.

As she turned to go back upstairs, something caught her eye. There'd been a flash of light in the empty first floor bedroom.

"Alanis?" Sloane called, tiptoeing into the door frame.

Alanis' ghost was not there, but the window was wide open again. The blinds shook with the breeze, and Sloane realized the open window was what had caused a breeze to flow through her house earlier.

"What the fuck?"

Sloane raced back to the front door and whipped it open, but Drew was already gone.

"Am I going insane?" Sloane wondered aloud. She was sure Jose had come out the front door. Had he come *in* through the back window?

She analyzed the room, but didn't see any dirt or footprints coming in. She snuck to the window and dared to peek out, but couldn't see the screen below the back wall anymore. Where had it been moved to?

"Could the wind have done it?"

She wished Alanis would return and answer some of her questions.

"I swear to god this day is too much," Sloane grumbled, shutting the window, and this time making sure it was locked from the inside.

#

"I probably left it open and forgot about it," Sloane told Jackson later. He'd come by to hand her a piece of mail in her name. It had an official government stamp.

Jackson eyed it suspiciously, but didn't ask, which Sloane appreciated. It was work-related, but if the government was going to trust their own mail system to deliver it to her house instead of her similarly named neighbor, it probably wasn't super high level.

"Maybe you did leave the window open. Still, you should be careful," he insisted.

"That's what Officer Byrd said earlier."

Jackson frowned.

Sloane looked out over his shoulder and yoinked Jackson inside her house.

"Nina," she whispered, closing the door quietly behind him.

"You really don't like her, do you?"

Sloane ignored the question and took the mail from him, putting it on her hall table. She carefully reached into the prop bowl and grabbed hold of her keys.

A corner of the prop bowl broke off.

Jackson dove for it, but she laughed and waved him off.

She removed one key from the set and handed it to him. "It's a mail key. Can you keep it for me? My mailbox is right below yours."

Jackson shrugged. "You sure you trust a presumed felon with your mail?"

"I think I'll survive," she laughed, releasing the key into his grip. "I have more spares upstairs. I give them to whomever will take one."

"I'm sure Nina would love one."

"Not her," Sloane huffed. "Now, speaking of your crimes, you'd better get out of here before Drew sees you."

Jackson's jaw dropped. "Hey! Presumed crimes!"

But Sloane noticed a twinge of agony on his face. *It must be hard to be suspected. It must be even harder to not know how to exonerate yourself.*

"Unless you'd like to stay for dinner," she added quickly. He was only a suspect, and the command to stay home was not a rule. It was just a suggestion.

"If you don't mind," Jackson replied. "It's lonely in the jail that is my house. Except for the ghosts, of course."

The nerves on Sloane's entire body lit up, but she quashed them down as she turned and went up the stairs. She hoped he wouldn't see her shock. Normal people joked about ghosts all the time. There was no way Jackson could see Alanis too, right? He would have said something.

But then again, *she* hadn't said anything.

At the top of the stairs, she looked for Alanis, but the apparition was gone again. Sloane took a deep breath and announced, "I'm just having Chinese again, I hope that's okay."

"My favorite," Jackson said, grabbing a box of takeout and an open bottle of wine. Sloane opened a drawer, took out some chopsticks, and handed Jackson a pair.

Jackson and Sloane stepped out onto her balcony, but almost immediately, Sloane gasped and stepped back inside.

"What the-" Jackson turned to look at her, but she darted her eyes to her left, indicating what she'd seen.

Just up the street, the black Bentley rolled through the shadows between the forest and Rick's house.

She pulled Jackson back inside and let the car pass between their houses. "I'm on to you," she whispered at it as it left the community.

She wasn't on to anything, of course. It was possible they were in fact just house hunting. After they'd driven away the other day and she'd pointed them out to Drew, she'd felt pretty foolish.

The car kept rolling and stopped in front of the unfinished first building. Sloane and Jackson moved back out onto the balcony and watched the car slow.

"Sorry," she said sheepishly. "I don't love new people."

Jackson also eyed the Bentley but forced a laugh. "Works for me, it means I get all your food and cookies."

"Well," Sloane scoffed at the car and dipped her chopsticks into chow mein. "If they're following one of us, they're doing a really piss poor job about hiding it."

Jackson followed her eyes to the car. "You think that guy is following you?"

"I don't know, I'm not even sure it's a guy."

"Oh, he's a guy alright. I almost hit him coming into the neighborhood the other day. I didn't expect anyone to drive out the service entrance of the neighborhood. I stared into his face when I was flipping him the bird."

"What did he look like?"

"I don't know, nondescript."

"Did he look like the type of guy who would buy a house here?"

"Do any of us look like the type of guy who would buy a house here? I don't know how to answer that question. I mean, there are a fair number of single people in this townhome community. Rick, Terra Mackleby, Officer Byrd, You, Myself."

"Yeah, but none of us drive Bentleys or wear suits."

"True. Realtor?"

"I thought about that, and Nina insists it is, but I'm not so sure. I just have this weird feeling about him."

"Well, we could go over there and talk to him."

"I'm not leaving my house, certainly not to talk to a stranger."

"I'll go, then. Don't eat my fried rice." Jackson went into the house and down the stairs. Sloane heard the front door open and close below her, and Jackson's footprints on the front stoop.

The Bentley softly roared to life, its brake lights flashing on before settling into drive. Again, it pulled out of the neighborhood and roared toward the highway. Sloane watched Jackson race out into the street between their houses and watch it leave.

He looked up at Sloane and shrugged. "'Fraidy cat."

"He saw you coming and was afraid you'd give him the finger again," Sloane laughed down at him. He flipped his middle finger up at her and she feigned panic and fear. He left the street and came back inside. She heard the sound of him locking the triple bolts, and she breathed a sigh of relief.

When Jackson got back upstairs and out on the balcony, Sloane said, "Whatever he's here for, he's definitely a wily sort. Doesn't get out of his car, drives away when we approach."

"He had his car started before I even got out the door," said Jackson. "He must have known we were watching him, and probably saw us talking about doing something about it."

"Do you think he was listening in, like with some listening device?"

Jackson thought about it. "Like with a giant reverse megaphone?"

"No, like what if someone came into my house and planted a listening device?"

"Who, like Jose?"

"Nah, never mind, I'm imagining things." Sloane laughed at herself. "Plus, who would be listening to me? I live alone and I have no enemies."

"Commie pinkos!"

"What even *is* a commie pinko?"

Jackson laughed. "No clue. But you know, there is a lot of dissent about just how much the government watches us, and how little freedom we have."

"The government is already watching us, we work for them," Sloane remarked. "Plus, if you want to talk about freedom, try being imprisoned in your house by your own mind. If the government is watching me—hell, even if the guy in the Bentley is watching me--their job is crazy easy. I don't leave. I have no secrets; save for the passwords I use to access dumb network stuff for the Feds. So, if the American government is interested in me, they're not going to find much beyond their own data."

"Maybe it's not the American government," Jackson offered.

She put her chopsticks in her lap and tilted her head. "This is crazy talk. But maybe I should double check my computer for spyware again, though."

"It never hurts." Jackson topped up Sloane's wine and traded his fried rice for her chow mein.

Sloane took another large swig of her drink, and the two of them sat in companionable silence. As the sun began to set, they watched the construction workers clear out for the evening. Many of them high-fived Jose as they departed, but as usual Jose didn't seem in a rush to leave for the day.

"He's harmless," Sloane said more to herself than to Jackson.

"So say we all," Jackson muttered.

Sloane ignored it, too focused on why Jose never seemed to leave. Why he was in her house. Could he be responsible for Alanis' death? Could Jackson?

After a moment, she spoke. "Someone needs to talk to the man in the Bentley. Maybe he knew Alanis and can get you off the hook."

"Shit," Jackson rubbed his forehead. "I probably shouldn't have given him the finger."

"We could try again this weekend," said Sloane.

"I can't, I'm heading to Kansas City tomorrow."

"Oh yeah? What's in Kansas City?"

"The funeral."

"Oh." Sloane bit her lip, not knowing what to say. So, she changed the topic back. "I'll get Charlie to talk to Bentley dude next time we see him. She can talk to anyone about anything."

CHAPTER THIRTY

As though she'd heard her name on the wind, Charlie came over the next morning before the brunch shift at the pub. Sloane filled her in on her next conquest: get the man in the Bentley to talk to her, without him seeing that she came from Sloane's house. Sloane told her the plan was for Charlie to wait in the woods and then come up with a reason to need his help.

"I can always play the damsel in distress," Charlie winked, as she snapped a heel off her four-inch Louboutin knockoffs.

"What are you doing?!" gasped Sloane.

"Don't worry about it, I've glued and reglued these a thousand times. They cost me ten bucks and are wonderful for picking up dudes, but I'm spoken so now, so they're useless."

Soon after coffee, Charlie put on her coat and broken shoe, and headed towards the gate to the forest path to wait. "Text me when his car pulls in."

"Be careful in the woods," Sloane said as Charlie slipped out the door into the chilled morning air.

"Be careful in your house," Charlie responded, her breath turning to mist as she stepped onto the sidewalk. "This cold will kill me before the neighborhood serial killer does."

Sloane laughed but felt uneasy. Perhaps this task was too much for Charlie to handle by herself. She wondered if the blood had come back positive as being Alanis', and if the killer had hid in the woods waiting for a so-called damsel in distress to attack. If so, were they still there? She wondered if Officer Byrd would be in the neighborhood today. Perhaps they should have waited and had him talk to the Bentley driver. Then again, the man in the Bentley had seen Drew already, with Sloane. He'd probably seen everyone in the neighborhood with her at some point.

After bolting the door and climbing the stairs, Sloane's phone beeped.

> Charlie: It's freezing out here.
>   Put some more coffee on.
>
> Sloane: You got it. Love you.
>
> Charlie: You'd better.

Sloane set up the coffee machine to run and stood by the balcony door, just behind the long sheers and out of view of the street. Sure enough, not a few minutes later the Bentley drove slowly into the neighborhood, slowed as it passed between Sloane and Jackson's house, and parked further up the street, towards the back fence where Charlie was perched.

> Sloane: He's here.
>
> Charlie: I'll give him a minute to
>   shut off his engine and get
>   comfortable.
>
> Sloane: Sounds good.
>
> Charlie: I covered my legs and
>   hands with dirt.

157

```
Sloane: What for? This isn't a
        camouflage mission!

Charlie: I'm playing a girl who
         stumbles out of the forest
         drunk from the night before.

Sloane: You're crazy.

Charlie: Acting!
```

As predictable, the Bentley driver shut off his engine and did not leave the car. Sloane watched, careful not to disturb the blinds in case he actually was watching her. She remained in the shadows of her darkened dining room.

A few minutes later, she spotted Charlie coming through the gate from the forest, stumbling. Sloane laughed. Charlie was overacting again, and her moves were unnecessary.

At the same time, Nina shot out from her house, jumping down the steps in twos and leaping into the Ford Escape parked in front of her house. Charlie saw this as well and paused to watch. Nina roared the engine and took off out the gates of the complex. The Bentley's engine also roared to life, but the driver was slower to pull out. Charlie ran towards his car to get a better look at his face as he angled his car and looked over his shoulder. Sloane wondered if he was following Nina or was just too shook up by the random women in the neighborhood acting strangely. She decided to also be a scary random woman, and she strode out onto the balcony in her bathrobe to watch the melee, trying to catch a look at the driver as he sped past her house. Charlie traversed the distance between the road and Sloane's house and came back inside.

Sloane handed her a warm coffee with a dash of cream, and Charlie removed her broken heels.

"Well, that failed," Sloane said to her, offering up the sugar bowl.

Charlie shook her head. "Not really, actually. It was very strange." She stared into her cup, stirring the cream into ghostly images and then folding it back out again.

"Strange, how?"

"I think the driver of that car was at the HOA meeting the other day."

"Principal Mackleby?"

"No, Ken. That quiet dude who lives with Nina."

#

Sloane's head was spinning. Why would Ken sit in a weird car all day trolling his own neighborhood? Why was Nina in a rush to get the hell out of the neighborhood and why did he follow? Was Ken a realtor? Why would Nina be secretive about that? Who are any of these people, anyway?

The women sat for a long time on the couch, mulling these things over in their heads.

"Married people are so strange," Sloane said the last two words slowly.

"It's probably some weird sex thing, right?" Charlie tried to lighten the conversation. Sloane laughed and made a face. A million thoughts were running through her head, but her friend could always find a joke somewhere.

"We should tell Drew. He's probably been wondering about that car."

"Hot. More action for the neighborhood sex game!" Charlie's eyes glowed.

"Stop making us fail the Bechdel test. I just think he should know. He's investigating a murder, you know."

"Speaking of which, I'd feel better if you moved closer to me in Fallstaff," Charlie said. "There are too many weirdos around here."

"I'm one of them," laughed Sloane. But Charlie was right. Everyone in her neighborhood was somehow just slightly *off*.

CHAPTER THIRTY-ONE

Weekends were the hardest on Sloane. As a consultant she could always work, but logging into the government sites on weekends wasn't necessary unless she was on call. Without anyone to talk to, Sloane often caught herself thinking and rethinking about the events of the past weeks. Sunday afternoon, she stood in her small tech office staring at a corkboard filled with post-it notes and pictures, trying to find connections. If no one was going to solve Alanis's murder, perhaps she'd give it a whirl.

The timelines seemed so bizarre. The neighborhood was new, so everyone was a brand-new resident. She wondered why Jackson felt he needed a roommate right away almost before getting settled himself. He'd moved in first, about a week before Sloane closed on her house, and two to three weeks before she moved in. The Pacillis and Smythes had moved in a week after her. Then Rick moved into the duplex next to Jackson's a week after them, shortly followed by Principal Mackleby next to the Smythes. Then there was Drew, who hadn't moved in yet.

Sloane, Mackleby, and Jackson were the only neighborhood residents without anyone in the duplex next to them, although the ones next to Jackson's and Mackleby's houses were finished, and the one next to Sloane's wasn't. On windy days, giant For Sale signs thumped from their respective empty balconies.

Sloane's ex, Brian, had been nice enough to drive her and her stuff across the state to move her in, while she'd hid from the world in the backseat of his SUV. The day she'd moved in, Alanis must have been moving her stuff into Jackson's basement room, and work was being completed on the second half of Jackson and Principal Mackleby's duplexes.

And then there was the first building in the neighborhood, the large duplex still completely under construction, although she was beginning to believe Jose lived there in secret. She was starting to think Charlie was right, and she should have a roommate of her own. If she could ever get a moment alone with him, she might invite Jose after all. She didn't need any rent money, but a friendly face to keep watch on the door--and that weird backyard window--would definitely come in handy.

But was he actually friendly? She wondered.

Rent money. Her mind came back to that. Why did Jackson take in Alanis? As a tech worker who bought his own house he must have money, Sloane guessed.

Occam's razor crossed her mind again. The simplest answer might be the truth. Jackson might be the killer.

She wished Alanis were around, and she went looking for the ghost.

Who was she? Jackson had said she was a troubled cousin, but what did that mean?

The move-in dates were all so close to each other.

And why was Ken hiding in a Bentley all day?

And had someone tampered with her computer? Her back window?

Was Sloane losing her mind?

CHAPTER THIRTY-TWO

In the early evening, after an afternoon staring at Doctor Who reruns while her brain jostled over senseless neighborhood data, Jackson's familiar shave-and-a-haircut knock sounded at the front door. Sloane bounded down to the front hall, happy to see him.

"I thought were heading to Kansas City today," she said as she whipped the door open.

Before her stood not Jackson, but Nina. Sloane froze in fright, not at the sight of her less than friendly neighbor, but because the shock of being wrong had caught her so off guard. She clutched a hand to her heart in panic before settling down to the new change of scene.

"Nina," she finally said. "I thought you were someone else."

"I learned his knock the other day when Jackson came to visit you. I thought using it would finally get you to answer the door."

"Nina, this isn't a great time," Sloane lied. Truthfully, she had nothing else to do. "As you can see, my laundry isn't out anymore."

"I was hoping I could borrow your Wi-Fi for a second." Nina flashed a laptop along with a large, dopey smile.

Sloane eyed the laptop. "You don't have Wi-Fi at your house?"

"It's not working," Nina frowned. "Stupid Cable company seems to be going down for everyone, but you've got fiber-optic, right? This was what I was talking about the other day. I just need to download a recipe my mother sent me. Do you mind?"

"You know, I'd actually better not, Nina. I-" Sloane stopped herself.

Was she being overprotective, or was it Nina, or Ken, who had tried to log onto her computer the last time?

"You know what, you can use a mobile hotspot," Sloane said.

"Mmm can't, it won't be fast enough. This recipe will only take a minute to download with your connection. Ken really wants his mom's chicken tonight. Men, right?"

"I thought-" Sloane stopped herself from saying I thought it was *your* mom. But it could be nothing. "Sure," she finally relented, "let me type my password in for you."

She took Nina's computer and saw that Nina had already opened her router name, JacksonS. She went to sit on the stairs, and as she did so she unclicked JacksonS and clicked on Leonardo and Francesca's router instead, Pac71. She typed in the password Francesca had given her the other day, praying Leonardo would forgive her, and she minimized the Wi-Fi window. She handed it back to Nina and prayed the woman wouldn't check to see which account she was actually logged into.

"You're all set. Do you want to come up and sit down while the recipe downloads?"

"Nah, your Wi-Fi signal stretches to my house. I'll just download it over there," Nina replied, then quickly added, "near all the ingredients. You know how cooking is."

Sloane frowned but tried to ignore how awkward and uncomfortable it felt. She was glad the Pacilli's internet was closer to the Smythe's house, so hopefully Nina's connection would stick and she wouldn't come back. She closed the door, wishing Nina a good night. Then she shut off the outside lights and went upstairs to bed.

Sloane decided sleep was more appealing than visiting with neighbors.

CHAPTER THIRTY-THREE

Monday morning found Sloane tossing and turning once more, images of ghosts and strangers and stolen Wi-Fi passwords fuzzed in her head. She shuddered as she crawled into the shower trying to wash the images away. With all the weirdness going on in her neighborhood, she expected that there would be many more nights of bad dreams, possibly for the rest of her life, or until she got help.

But who can help me when I'm afraid of everything?

She chose not to slip into her comfy bathrobe, instead wearing thick layers and a pair of faded jeans. She took a coffee out on her balcony with a sharp, fitted jacket instead, wanting to show the world that she was functional and capable, and nobody could get her.

Jackson opened his door and looked toward Officer Byrd's house, before coming out onto the street and calling up to her.

"I came back last night but your lights were off. Did you go to bed early?"

"Your knock has been discovered and abused," Sloane said back to him. "I had to avoid the door."

Jackson threw his hands on his hips and stole a glance around the neighborhood. "Those jerks. I'll come up with a new one."

He crossed the street and Sloane went downstairs to let him in. While he patted a weird drumroll onto the door, she grabbed the rest of the set of keys from the prop bowl. As she opened the door, she handed it to him.

"What's this," he looked down at the chain. On it was her house key and a bottle opener in the shape of a red unicorn.

"Just take it," Sloane brushed him off and turned to head upstairs. "I don't leave the house anyway and every time I reach for the key, I break that stupid bowl again."

"I'm not taking keys to your house," Jackson followed, trying to offer the house key to her ascending backside.

"Forming a special knock is not going to help me discern who is at my door anymore, not with strangers in the neighborhood watching your every movement. Nina probably heard today's poor drumroll."

Jackson huffed, "Hey, I threw a cymbal shake in there too, that's hard to master in knock form."

Sloane laughed, and he looked down at the keys. "I'll get these copied, *one* copy, and give this back to you, okay? But I'm nervous about there being too many copies of your keys out there."

"How safe am I, Jackson?" Sloane spun around to face him on the main level. She waved her hands around her. "People are busting into and out of my house at random, anyway. A goddamn screen window disappeared. What does having keys matter? Alanis wasn't safe." Sloane turned back around and moved toward the balcony window, eyeing the street.

Jackson followed. "Alanis left the house and went god knows where to do who knows what. You don't do that." He took her chin in his hand and led her gaze away from the window. "You can trust me," he whispered as he tilted her chin up to his.

Sloane took a second to register what was happening, then broke into a full laugh.

Jackson fumed for a second, and then broke into a laugh of his own. "Hey, I was trying to be sexy and comforting."

"You're a nut," she said, and grabbed his face with both of her palms. She drew her mouth up to his and captured his lips with hers. Before Jackson could fully realize what was happening and return the smooch, she withdrew.

A vaguely familiar heat ran through her body and caught her off guard. It had been a long time.

She removed her hands from his face and, not having anything else to do with them, stuck them in her pockets and rocked herself up on her toes. She composed her blush, smiled quickly, and turned toward the kitchen.

Jackson temporarily froze in place, his mouth curved into a kiss shape, then he relaxed. "That was supposed to be *my* surprise kiss."

Sloane busied herself with the coffee maker to hide her pink cheeks. "Listen, Jackson, I'm—" she chose her words carefully, "-not sure I can get involved with anyone right now."

Jackson followed her and grabbed two mugs out of the cabinet. "With anyone, or with me?"

Sloane sighed and turned to him. "Drew said it could upset the investigation."

"Drew can suck my left nut."

There was a temporary pause while Sloane considered this option, then she giggled.

"Let me cook up some eggs and we'll have breakfast on the balcony," Jackson offered, scouring the fridge for random ingredients.

"Sometimes I wonder if you just come over here because I have food."

"Hey, I don't keep these awesome things in my fridge," he said, pulling out a green pepper and flipping it in his hand.

"Ah, a bachelor. Let me guess, your fridge has a twelve pack of beer, an expired container of milk, and a leftover sandwich from a sub shop."

"You're close. The twelve pack is almost empty now. I need to restock."

#

Jackson concocted a deliciously mouth-watering egg scramble, and they toasted their breakfast to the Gods of culinary arts. The street was quiet, and although there were no cloud blankets shading the scary, expansive sky, Sloane felt safe with the good food and company. She said as much to Jackson as they scraped egg off their plates.

"What's the process like? For recovery," Jackson asked.

"From agoraphobia? Immersion therapy is really the only way to help it."

"So why aren't you pushing yourself to leave the house more often?"

"What are you talking about? This past week I've all but lived outdoors," Sloane stated. But she took some time to really think about it. "Convenience, I guess. This world is so easy to ignore. I can get food delivered, clothes, appliances, books, everything. I have no need to leave anymore. I bet if I tried, I could find a traveling doctor, too. Hell, I interviewed and got this government gig over Zoom. I don't need to go anywhere, so until this week my feeling was -- why attack a problem that isn't there?"

"Until this week," Jackson agreed. "So now have you finally realized you need to practice going outside?"

Sloane thought about it. She didn't really have an answer, she just knew it was time to finally leave the roost, and that things were going to get even weirder and possibly more dangerous if she stayed. "Well, now I have this cute little flirtation with you," she said to him. She took his plate and stood to bring it back into the kitchen. As she did, she added, "And you may need to be bailed out of jail at some point. I'd better practice so I can make it to the precinct one day."

Jackson laughed, but a brief look of terror flashed in his eyes.

Sloane patted his shoulder. "More coffee," she offered her hand for his mug.

"Thanks," he said, and followed her in from the balcony. "Actually," Jackson stopped her as she approached the coffee machine, "I want you to come over and have coffee at my house."

Sloane froze "What? Why?"

Jackson pointed at some tchotchkes on Sloane's shelves. "I like your decor. I need you to do this for my house, too."

"Didn't Alanis decorate your house at all?"

"She mainly stuck to herself downstairs. She didn't touch my space at all."

Sloane felt her heart speed up. Panic, not lust, she thought. She stumbled a bit over what to say. "This isn't really decor; I just have a lot of time on my hands. I'm sure I can't help you."

Sloane was searching desperately for excuses now, and she knew it.

Jackson wasn't accepting it. "Come on, it'll be just like going to Nina's house."

"Nina's house is next door, and if you recall, that was extremely difficult for me, and I had two of you to help. You're asking me to cross a street. A large, wide street with parking on both sides and cars rushing by."

"They're hardly rushing at five miles per hour. Come on, I'll hold you the entire way."

"You're going to have to carry my screaming body."

"So be it, let's go." He took her hand and pulled her down the stairs.

"I could consider this coercion or something. I'll call the police."

"It's immersion therapy. I'll call your psychotherapist and it'll all be explained away." Jackson grabbed her jacket from the coat hook where it hung unused. A layer of dust was evident along the lapel. He gently blew it off and put it around her shoulders. As he unbolted each door lock, her heart raced increasingly at exponential speeds. As the knob was turned and the door opened, a bead of sweat formed at her hairline, and dripped down her temple.

"I'm a mess, Jackson. I'm a mess."

Jackson paused, then started to close the door again. "Okay. No pressure," he said. "We can try again another day."

"No." Sloane released a breath. "Wait."

Jackson watched her for a moment. Then he reopened the door a tiny inch and peered out through the crack. "I won't make you do anything, but honestly it's less than ten seconds, Sloane. I've timed it. If we run right now we can be at my door before anyone even knows where we've gone. I don't see anyone out there right now."

"What about Bentley guy?"

He stuck his head further out, "Okay, he's there but honestly I'm not sure he's a threat."

"Well, he's about to get the surprise of his life, because I'm going to sweat and puke all over your front porch."

"It's supposed to rain tomorrow, the weather will be my cleaning lady. Come on."

"Okay."

He grabbed her arm and pulled her outside. He threw one hand around her back and clasped her flailing arm with the other, forcing her to move with him onto the porch and down the steps.

"Don't scream," he chillingly whispered in her ear. But she couldn't scream even if she tried, her voice was frozen.

A million thoughts ran through her head. *How do I get home? What happens if his door is locked?*

An even more chilling thought flashed in her mind, as well. *If he's guilty, then he's leading helpless me into his house and no one will know I'm there.* She pushed it out of her head and ran with him. She didn't even turn her head to look at the guy in the Bentley. She just fell loose into Jackson's arms and let him pull her all the way across and up onto his porch.

"Look, I left the door unlocked," Jackson grinned, seeming to read her mind. "You're safe!" He opened the door and pulled her inside. She collapsed onto the floor, trying to catch her breath and slow her own heart. Jackson sat on the stairs while she came around. She took in her surroundings from the cold tiled floor. Jackson's floorplan was supposed to be the reverse of hers, a mirror image, but his was rearranged. Alanis's room faced the front, not the back.

The door to her room was open, and Sloane could see that the police had torn it apart during their investigation. Books and boxes lay strewn around the floor. A desk sat under the window, and Sloane could see where Alanis used to peek out at her late at night.

Unlike in her own house, Sloane did not feel Alanis' presence at all. The room was empty and cold, as if it was never her home whatsoever

"This floor is laid out differently," Sloane said aloud.

"It's an older elevation. The main floor is similar, except my balcony is at the back facing the highway. Then it's reversed again on the top floor. My bedroom faces your house, and my laundry and office are at the back. Come see!" Jack held out his hand for Sloane to grab, but she remained on the floor. She needed another minute of hearing his voice in order to recover.

"So, you can watch me in my house from your bedroom?"

Jackson laughed. "I promise there isn't much to see unless you're out on your balcony. Perhaps Alanis watched you, too."

She absolutely did and still does, Sloane wanted to say. Instead, she frowned. "I feel bad that one of the last things she saw while alive was me hanging my laundry out on my balcony. I hope she wasn't as upset with that behavior as Nina was."

"I'm sure that was the last thing on her mind. She didn't strike me as the sort to care about esthetics. She barely even decorated her room." Jackson eyed the bedroom wistfully, as though searching for something that wasn't there. "In fact, she had very little possessions. She just needed a room, so I rented it to her."

"But you didn't need the money," Sloane stated more than asked. She looked again into Alanis's room. A few stray papers remained on the floor, and the cot had been stripped clean. "What happened to all of her stuff?"

"Again, there wasn't much," he said, "but the CIA came and rifled through it."

"The CIA? What kind of a murder investigation needs to involve the CIA? Are you talking about the FBI?"

"Oh geez, I have no idea anymore," Jackson shook his head. "But when someone from the upper echelons of government comes to your door, you don't ask questions, you just let them do their business. I was too scared to try and monitor what they were doing."

Sloane nodded and backed away from the room, trying to consider all the things she was looking at and the strange data she'd been given. *Why would the CIA come in? Who was this woman?* Sloane took Jackson's hand, the one he'd been holding out for her patiently, and they climbed the stairs into his kitchen.

"It's disconcerting to be in a house that is kind of like mine but yet not at all. I feel a little dizzy." She told him.

"You feel dizzy because I just forced you outside. I'm sure the space will grow on you."

Sloane felt herself relax. "How long are you planning to keep me hostage?"

"You're free to leave anytime," Jackson laughed, and held his hand out through the dining room window toward her house.

"You're a jerk." She pushed him against the kitchen island and pounded on his chest, laughing the entire time. "You have no intention of helping me get home today."

"I just said I'd help you get over here! Nobody said anything about bringing you home." He grabbed her in a big bear hug.

She leaned up to kiss him, but a scream from the street shook the dining room window. Sloane recognized the sound from the night Alanis was killed.

"But Alanis is in my house," she whispered, dropping Jackson and running to the window.

Jackson froze, momentarily puzzled, then followed her. "What are you talking about?"

Nina stood in the street outside Sloane's house, her hands on her face. Sloane jumped back from Jackson's window and pulled him with her, to stay out of Nina's sight.

"What are you -"

"Shush," Sloane said to Jackson, holding him back from the view. "Something isn't right here. Wait a minute."

She tried to recall events from the night of the death. If Alanis was not the one to scream, then Nina was there, or at least awake, and that means Sloane hadn't heard Alanis scream at all.

I could be wrong, however. I could always be wrong.

But she wasn't. Not this time. This time things started to fall into place. If Nina was the screamer, then Jackson running out of his house that night wasn't so confusing after all. And the blood behind her house that was marked as Alanis's suddenly made sense - because she didn't die where the noise was coming from, she died elsewhere.

But was that actually Nina's scream the night of the murder, or was she being honest when she said she slept through it? Nina sleeping through anything seemed highly suspect.

Jackson watched Sloane running scenarios through her head and held his finger to his mouth while he peeked out the window to look for Nina. She was gone.

They both sat down at his 1950s style dining room table, it's cold plastic surface sending chills through Sloane's body. Or perhaps it wasn't the table at all.

She told Jackson her concerns.

Jackson nodded. "Her blood was found behind your house, and her body indicated she'd been dragged to my car, but the scream came later and from a direction we could both hear it from, we agree there. And yet none of us saw anything that night, until the car was opened the next day."

They remained seated, staring at each other's hands for longer than necessary, their heartbeats slowing. She felt guilt for considering him a suspect, but she didn't tell him as much. She still had too much to think about. She stepped back and walked to his couch. He followed her to the living room and found her a blanket. "This is very overwhelming, Jackson."

"Would you like to go home?" He seemed genuinely concerned and sat down near enough to comfort her on the sofa, but not smother her. She appreciated that. She was beginning to feel nervous again.

A fast and angry knock sounded on Jackson's door, followed by Nina yelling muffled noises through the solid panel. Sloane put a finger to her neck to indicate that she wasn't there, and Jackson nodded. Sloane did not need the extra stress of Nina's opinions on why she was in Jackson's house. She was still trying to recover and piece together what she knew.

Jackson flew down the stairs to answer the door.

Sloane heard muffled chatter, followed by Nina's high pitched angry voice. She heard her name at least three times, but remained where she was. Could Nina be trusted if she were so willing to lie to the police? She knew Jackson could hide his emotion, but Sloane could not. She'd start accusing Nina and it would be all over.

She heard the muffled sounds growing louder, and Nina's harsh voice climbing the stairs. It was over. She formulated her thoughts.

Nina spotted her in the living room and pointed fingers "You're here! Are you safe? What has this man done to you?"

"I'm fine, Nina. What do you want?"

"I saw your door was ajar, and I went into your house, and that repairman was in there again, so I panicked!"

"The entire community heard you panic." Sloane started toward the dining room window, trying to remain calm. "Jose is in my house?"

"I'll go check it out," Jackson stated, and he ran down the stairs. Sloane heard his door slam.

She tried to follow him, but Nina stepped in front of her and pointed a finger at her chest. "I thought you had a mental disorder," she accused.

Sloane sighed. "It's an anxiety disorder."

"Six of one..."

"Nina, I'm concerned about you," Sloane said.

"You're concerned about *me*? I'm concerned about *you*! I'm just trying to be a good neighbor. When someone is missing, I want to know about it."

"I'm not missing! And why did you go into my house just now? That doesn't seem weird to you?"

"No, and thank goodness I did, because that repairman was in there again! I went in because I was suspicious when I saw your front door open. After you gave me the wrong IP yesterday, I got confused."

"What do you mean *again*?" Had Jose been in her house like she'd thought? But how would Nina know? Sloane shook her head. "*You're* confused? What happened the night Alanis was murdered?"

An odd flash swept across Nina's brow, but she recovered quickly. "I don't know what you're talking about. I told the police what happened that night."

"But I know something about you that they don't," Sloane said. She walked around to one side of the kitchen island, away from Nina. "I feel like I should bring them this new information."

"You don't know anything," stated Nina. She moved around the kitchen island toward Sloane.

Sloane backed around the other way. "You were there, Nina. You screamed on that night. That was your scream, it wasn't Alanis!"

"Oh please, Sloane. You can't prove I wasn't nestled in my bed at three in the morning."

"Then how did you know what time the murder took place?"

"How did *you* know what time the murder took place? Where were you, Sloane? Is this problem of yours just a ruse to slaughter innocent people? Are you and Mr. Stone in this together, killing people for sport?"

"That's absurd," Sloane laughed.

"But it's what everyone will think, until they find your body."

"What are you talking about?"

Before Sloane could register what was happening, Nina had pulled a knife out from the back of her jeans and scooted over the counter.

"What the f-" Sloane screamed.

"Shut up," Nina held the knife up to Sloane's neck. "Give me the password, Ms. Jackson."

Had she just developed an accent?

Sloane's head was spinning. "The password?"

"Yes, you moron!"

Sloane felt a sharp pain and a short gush of blood drip down her neck, as Nina pressed the knife against her ear.

"My-" Sloane tried to breathe. The pressure of Nina's elbow on her neck was hurting her windpipe.

"Yes. Your password, for the government access, you fucking imbecile!"

"It was you, in my house-" Sloane tried to stall, hoping Jackson would return. She doubted Jose was in her house. It would only take Jackson a few seconds to figure that out, she was sure.

"Of course it was me! But you and your stupid disease kept you homebound, so I was never able to get in there," Nina screeched. "Then the one time you were at Francesca's that asshole repairman happened to come in."

"So you tried to look around on my server instead—" Sloane couldn't finish the thought, as Nina pressed the knife deeper into her skin. Her eyes darted toward the staircase, willing someone to come save her.

"If you think Jackson is coming back, he's not. At least not *awake*, anyway. Ken will take care of him."

"Ken?" Sloane panicked.

"Yes, my stupid fake husband Ken. He's been in your house, too. Now give me the password or you both will lose it."

Suddenly things became irrationally and instantly clear to Sloane. Alanis walked everywhere, so had cut through the forest on her way home. In the dark, Nina might even have said "Sloane" and Alanis heard "Stone," her last name, and acknowledged it. Then she was murdered in Sloane's yard. When Nina shoved the body in the car, trying to make Jackson look guilty, she may have seen movement in Sloane's house and realized she had the wrong person, then screamed.

Nina watched her as she thought. "You're figuring it out? Good job. You could be a spy too if you weren't dead."

"But I'm just an admin person," Sloane sputtered softly.

"For the fucking Federal Government! You have top clearance and you've never fucking done anything with it except order agents new passports, you scaredy-cat piece of shit. If you won't give me the password I'll figure out another way to get in. Now your body will be found here and when your boyfriend recovers, he'll be locked up for good—" Nina raised the knife and aimed it at Sloane's heart.

Sloane inhaled and closed her eyes.

Just then, she felt a powerful and cold breeze between the two of them. She opened her eyes and felt the spirit of Alanis in the room with them. Nina looked momentarily puzzled, the knife still held loosely in the air. She seemed to shake her head, then snarled again.

Alanis's ghost blew between them again, making Nina's hair flash forward into her eyes.

Sloane pushed as hard as she could, and Nina stumbled backward toward Jackson's granite countertop. Alanis blew past her one more time, causing her to trip wildly. Sloane heaved one more time and Nina's head thumped against the granite countertop.

"Miss Sloane," she heard from the foyer below.

"Jose? Is that you? Hurry!"

She pinned Nina on the ground. Blood spurted from the woman's head, but she was still breathing. She heard Jose lumbering up the stairs behind her. He saw the mess and grabbed some twine from his toolbelt, tying Nina up.

Sloane stood and looked around her. Alanis's ghost was gone. "Thank you Alanis," she whispered. "Wherever you are."

After tying Nina up, Jose stood and held out an arm for Sloane to hold on to. "You are okay, miss Sloane?"

Sloane took a deep breath. "Yes, Jose. I'm glad you got here when you did." Her eyes went wide, realizing he might not have any idea what was happening. "Let me explain-"

"It's okay, miss, I heard some of it," Jose held a hand up. Then he spotted the wound under her ear. He grabbed a paper towel from Jackson's counter, and she let him hold it against her neck. When he pulled it back, there was still fresh blood. "This is pretty bad, miss Sloane."

Sloane panicked. "Where is Jackson?" She took the paper towel from him, and ran to the sink to get it wet.

"Senor Stone is on top of Senor Smythe."

Sloane stared back at him for a moment. "In another world, that might be kind of hot," She gasped at herself, not quite sure her brain was functioning correctly.

Jose and Sloane double-checked Nina's body. She was alive, just unconscious.

"I can't be deported," Jose whispered, more to himself than to Sloane.

"You only helped. I'm the one who bashed her head in," Sloane laughed. "Come on, let's go help Jackson."

Jose led Sloane out across the street. Although she grasped his arm quite tightly, she felt a little less overwhelmed by the outside world and the living and the dead within it.

Back in her own foyer, Jackson sat atop Ken, pinning him down. "This idiot tried to knock me out with your nice glass bowl," he waved at the broken glass around them.

Sloane laughed. "Dammit, that stupid thing is so hard to put back together!"

CHAPTER THIRTY-FOUR

Within minutes of the police arriving, the black Bentley was towed and the CIA identified themselves.

"It seemed Ken was just a lookout," one of the agents told Sloane. "He literally sat in that car watching the neighborhood until you left, and then either he or Nina would try to sneak in and break into your computer."

"Sounds like the most boring job on the planet," Sloane laughed. She sat on her front steps, the nerves of being outside taking a backseat to the exhaustion almost being murdered.

Two guys lugged Ken's unconscious body out from behind her, and she scooted out of the way so they could move past. Jackson followed them out and sat beside Sloane, resting an arm around her back for support. She leaned into him, grateful.

After Ken was secure in the back of a truck, more suits went into Jackson's house, presumably to retrieve Nina. Despite the woman being a homicidal secret spy, Sloane hoped she was alive.

"These two weren't a real couple," the CIA agent continued. "We think they were hired by some foreign entity, and for whatever reason they targeted you to get into the most secure government servers."

"I wonder how they found me," Sloane all but whispered.

"Same way I did, I bet," Jackson said. "Just poking around. Then, when you applied for a mortgage on your new house they might have seen your address. Or maybe they looked at divorce documents. Who knows."

A police unit drove into the neighborhood, lights flashing, and Officer Byrd stepped out of the passenger seat of one of the cars.

The CIA agent flashed his ID and said, "we got this," as Drew approached.

"I'm here for her," Drew huffed. "Are you okay?" He looked at Sloane and frowned at Jackson.

Jackson squeezed Sloane a little tighter, making Sloane blush. *Men.*

"I'm fine, Drew. Thanks."

Drew coughed. "After talking with the Feds," he side-eyed the agent, "We think we figured out how it all went down. Not knowing quite what you looked like at the time, Nina and Ken – assuming that's their real names – couldn't confirm that Alanis was you. Alanis may have fought back, causing Nina to kill her. The feds assume Nina murdered her by accident, possibly trying to get login credentials that Alanis didn't have. Either way, if Alanis had been you, the two of them would have then snuck into your house and stolen your tech."

"But I was just an admin," Sloane repeated quietly. She shuddered. "Poor Alanis."

The CIA raised an eyebrow at her. He obviously knew her 'admin' work was more important than she was letting on, but he kept his mouth shut.

"Damn," Jackson let go of her back. "It's my fault, then. Because my name is so similar to Sloane's."

"We don't know that for sure," the agent said, but Sloane thought she saw Drew's head nod.

She wasn't going to let two men fight over who had got someone else killed. In the end, it was her own fault. She was the high-clearance federal employee.

Drew continued, "we found tons of evidence of tampering at your backyard window and downstairs bedroom, too."

"They could have come in any time and murdered me. No one would know." Sloane whispered, "And Alanis warned me every time."

"What's that?" Both Jackson and Drew raised an eyebrow. It looked good on them.

"Nothing," Sloane shook her head, remembering when Alanis told her to go outside. That was probably when Ken was removing the back window pain. And every time Alanis said Nina's name. Was she telling her who had killed her? *You saved my life*, Sloane looked to the sky.

They watched the other suits drag Nina out of Jackson's house. Sloane was relieved the woman appeared to still be alive. "Thank goodness she tripped or whatever and you were able to regain control," Jackson said.

More like, thank goodness Alanis hung around to avenge her own death, Sloane wanted to say aloud, but couldn't.

"Where is Jose?" Jackson looked up and down the street.

"We'd like to talk to him," the agent said. "We just need a statement to find out how much he heard. It helps to corroborate your story."

Sloane looked both ways up the street, then back at her own duplex. "I know where he is, but I need confirmation that he won't be questioned about anything besides what happened today." She eyed the agent, hoping he got the hint.

"We deal with international threats, ma'am. We don't give two shits about what customs and immigration might be interested in."

Sloane nodded and stood. She only wobbled a bit before she descended her front steps.

Drew reached out a hand to steady her.

Jackson stood too, and asked, "Want me to come with?"

"No gents," Sloane laughed. "I got this."

She descended her steps and walked the five yards to the steps of the townhome connected to hers. She held onto the railing as she climbed up. Then she knocked lightly at the door. Through a glass window she could see the duplex was almost finished inside, but still hauntingly empty of furniture.

She watched Jose descend the stairs carefully, and she waved at him.

When he opened the door, her first words were, "Why doesn't my side of the building have this glass window?"

Jose chuckled, but he seemed nervous, too. His eyes darted around behind her.

"You're not in trouble," Sloane whispered. "You helped us."

Jose poked his head out the door and saw Drew, Jackson, and the federal agent staring back at him. "I'm not supposed to be in here" he said.

Sloane nodded. She'd had a feeling Jose had been living next to her illegally, sometimes in the townhouse abutting hers, and sometimes in the unfinished duplexes next to them. It explained the occasionally flickering lights. No ghosts in there, just a guy who needed a break.

"I have a free room in my basement," Sloane said to him. "I'd love to have a roommate to answer the door to these types," she nodded over her shoulder at the three dudes behind her.

"You're serious?" Jose smiled.

"Of course. You helped save my life a few times," Sloane insisted. She'd love the extra support and, judging by how quiet Jose had been as he'd squatted next door to her for these past weeks, she could tell he'd be a friendly and quiet roommate.

"This is Jose," she introduced the builder to the three men. "He lives with me."

Jackson and Drew eyed her with suspicion but didn't say anything.

As promised, the federal agent didn't ask for proof of Jose's identification, he just wanted to ask a few questions. The two of them walked together out into the street, and approached the car Nina and Ken were shoved into. She appeared to be awake.

When she saw Jose, Nina swore at him. "Homeless bum!"

"Not homeless," smiled Jose and waved at the collection of duplexes. "Not when I build so many homes!"

On Sloane's front step, Drew frowned and shuffled his feet. "If you don't need any more assistance, miss Jackson,"

"Please call me Sloane, Drew. We're neighbors. I think we can be on a first-name basis."

Jackson put an arm around Sloane's back again, as if claiming his territory. Sloane rolled her eyes. He offered the officer a handshake. "Thanks for watching out for our little neighborhood, Drew-"

"*You* call me Officer Byrd, Mr. Stone. I've still got my eye on you." Drew growled. But he took Jackson's hand and shook it, before stepping toward the curb.

"Cool it, silly boys," Sloane admonished them. "And go home, both of you. I'll come by both your houses with cookies later. I owe you both that much."

Then she turned on her heels and went back inside her house, alone.

CHAPTER THIRTY-FIVE

The following few days were quiet, and lonely. Alanis' ghost never returned, and Sloane presumed that their time was through. Jose kept to himself and went next door to work throughout the day.

Sloane got used to spending mornings on her balcony, the nervousness had all but disappeared. While she wasn't yet able to comfortably leave the entire house, she was glad the balcony no longer terrified her.

A few mornings later, Leonardo's Prius turned into the neighborhood. He parked in front of Sloane's house.

On the street next to the car, Sloane watched as the shape of a woman slowly apparated. She gasped.

Is it a ghost? Oh no, has Francesca passed?

Sloane wasn't afraid, she was terrified, but not of the apparition itself, just of what it might mean.

"Hi, Sloane," Leonardo got out of his car and waved up at her. He was smiling and chipper. The ghost continued to thicken, and it floated next to him, scowling.

"Hi Leonardo," Sloane said carefully.

The apparition fully formed, still translucent but it was easier to make out the features. Whoever this woman was, she was heftier, older looking. She didn't look like Francesca.

Sloane's shoulders relaxed. "Is everything okay?"

"Yes, yes! Thank you, Miss Sloane! It was scary, but Francesca and the baby are recovering well and should be home later this week. I came home to get her some fresh spices. Hospital food is-" Leonardo made a face and spat "-yucky."

Sloane laughed. "What's the baby's name?"

Leonardo crossed his arms over his chest and huffed. The ghost appeared to almost float right into him, but he didn't notice or flinch at all. Sloane wondered how much will and energy Alanis' soul had required to move Nina in those final moments.

Leonardo shook his head. "No name yet. We can't agree."

"Lizbet," an echo sounded from the ghost's direction. It was a smooth, lovely Italian voice. Once again, the lips didn't move, but the apparition turned its head to stare directly into Sloane's eyes. "Lizbet."

Sloane nodded ever so slightly. She said, "I really think you should name it Lizbet."

"Did Francesca tell you that? Oddio!" He scoffed. "Fine. I guess she did just suffer a difficult delivery." His shoulders relaxed and he sighed, shaking his head. "Lizbet was her mother's name. That damn woman and I didn't get along at all, god rest her soul." He crossed himself, then pointed at the sky. "Fine. Fine fine fine. You win for the last time, Lizbet!"

Leonardo shook his head again and stomped into his house.

The ghost of Lizbet seemed to smile. Then it disappeared.

Sloane laughed. *As far as solving ghost mysteries go, that one was easy.*

"Bring it on, spirits. I'm ready for you," she said into the wind.

THE END

<<<<>>>>

About the Author

Emmy Tidning lives in a magical fantasy world called the Pacific Northwest, where anything is possible but no one is real. She has four cats, a dog, a husband, some kids, and a widowed crow she befriended using peanuts. Emmy reads Tarot card, writes cosy romantic fun, and can be reached through the publisher at info@applieddivination.com

Find us on Facebook https://www.facebook.com/EPdivination
Instagram https://www.instagram.com/applieddivination/
And Twitter https://twitter.com/AppliedTarot

Acknowledgments

This book would not be possible without:
1) Ghosts.
2) Paranormal women's fiction writing tips, and tons of Zoom conference calls, with author TJ Deschamps. Check out the Midlife Olympians series!
3) The love and support from my family

Also Published by Applied Divination

Applied Tarot
Applied Runes
Psychic Word Puzzles
Applied Tarot Reversed
Applied Tasseography
Faye's Fortune
Charlie's Chill

Visit applieddivination.com for more information.

Now available from Applied Divination

Applied Tasseography

A Practical Guide to Interpreting Tea Leaves

What movie should you watch when a dog shows up at the bottom of your cup?

You should watch the **Truman Show!**

I will never not recommend The Truman Show.

Follow emilypaper.com for more information!

www.ingramcontent.com/pod-product-compliance
Lightning Source LLC
Chambersburg PA
CBHW060814120626
46557CB00001B/217